Money-Makin' Mamas

D0057267

Money-Makin' Mamas

Silk Smooth

www.urbanbooks.net

Urban Books, LLC
97 N18th Street
Wyandanch, NY 11798

Money-Makin' Mamas

Copyright © 2016 Silk Smooth

All rights reserved. No part of this book may be reproduced in any form or by any means without prior consent of the Publisher, except brief quotes used in reviews.

ISBN 13: 978-1-62286-781-3
ISBN 10: 1-62286-781-5

First Mass Market Printing November 2016
First Trade Paperback Printing May 2016
Printed in the United States of America

10 9 8 7 6 5 4 3 2 1

This is a work of fiction. Any references or similarities to actual events, real people, living or dead, or to real locales are intended to give the novel a sense of reality. Any similarity in other names, characters, places, and incidents is entirely coincidental.

Distributed by Kensington Publishing Corp.
Submit Orders to:
Customer Service
400 Hahn Road
Westminster, MD 21157-4627
Phone: 1-800-733-3000
Fax: 1-800-659-2436

Money-Makin' Mamas

Silk Smooth

Part One

Introduction

Taffy Douglas

Chapter One

I haven't always been that bitch, but when a woman hooks up with a no-good-ass nigga, it be that way sometimes. That's exactly what I did, and my life hasn't been the same ever since. See, there was a time when I just sat back and kept my mouth shut. There was a time when I would let the nigga in my life call all the shots. There was a time when I would bow down, give that nigga head and fuck him from sun up to sun down. But then, one day it happened. Everything changed. His life and mine. After that, I became the woman I was destined to be . . . Taffy Douglas.

The year was somewhere around the late 1980s. I was only twenty-seven years old. I can't exactly recall the day and time, but I will never forget what that muthafucka Raysheed, a.k.a. Ray, had done. For years, he had gotten away with so much shit. My dumb, naïve ass had let him, and it was just a matter of time before I decided to stand up for myself. Truthfully, I didn't even know that I had it in me. I was a quiet, weak bitch who was too afraid to open my mouth and speak up when I felt something was wrong. Ray knew he'd had a fool. He was able to do anything his heart desired. I mean, the nigga was so good at what he did that it wasn't nothing for him to bring one of his hoes to the crib and fuck her right in front of me. And what did I do about it? Nothing. I lay right in the bed next to him while he fucked a Caucasian chick right beside me.

"What in the fuck are you lookin' at?" Ray yelled at me.

The woman's pale legs were thrown over his broad shoulders. He tore into her shit like he was tenderizing a piece of tough meat. I thought it was fish from the way her pussy smelled, but I sat there with my lips clamped tight. My eyes were wide, but I narrowed them after Ray yelled at me.

"Nothing, Ray. I . . . I just don't understand why you couldn't do this in another room."

"Bitch, this is my muthafuckin' bed! I pay the bills here, not you. If you don't like what I'm doin', too goddamn bad. And once I'm done, you can take yo' ass in the livin' room with them nappy-head-ass kids of yours."

Hell no, I didn't like it, and I didn't want to wait until he was done. I tossed the cover aside, but as I got ready to get out of the bed, Ray grabbed me by the back of my hair. He pulled my hair so tight and held me down on the bed. My eyes watered; my scalp felt as if it was bleeding.

"You move when I tell you to move!" he shouted. "Now, lie the fuck back down and learn somethin'."

I was too afraid to open my mouth. I knew what Ray's punches felt like, and I damn sure didn't feel like catching a beat down tonight.

"Raymond, darling," the prissy Southern woman said. She was a fat and nasty-looking bitch with dirty-blond hair flowing midway down her back "Must you be so mean to that girl? She only wants to watch. There ain't nothing wrong with her watching us, is there? Hell, she may even want to join us."

She giggled. I shot a dirty look in her direction, just to make her aware that I wasn't down with her plan and that she had fucked up Ray's name. He released his grip on my hair and slowly removed the woman's legs from his shoulders. His eyes were wider than mine. The look on his face appeared worse than death.

"You funky cock bitch! What in the hell did you just call me? I told you my name is Raysheed, Ray muthafuckin' McWilliams. Where in the hell did you get Raymond from? Do you think you can just make up any goddamn name for me, like they did Kunta Kinte? Y'all muthafuckas wanted to call him Toby, and now you want me to be Raymond. I got yo' damn Raymond all right. Here he is."

I witnessed fire in Ray's eyes as he raised his fist and slammed it right into the woman's beet-red face. Something cracked. Thick blood splattered—splattered on me. Ray kept beating the woman as if she had called him a black-ass nigger. As she screamed and hollered, I eased away from them and ran off into the living room with my girls. My whole body trembled; my legs were weak. I fell on the couch and held all three of my girls in my arms, mainly Simone who was just a baby. All of them were tearful as ever. The oldest one, Chyna, questioned what was going on.

"Who is in there, Mama? What's all that noise?" she softly whispered then shielded her ears from all the ruckus she heard.

I didn't want Ray to come out of the bedroom and say anything to us, so I told Chyna to lie back down and be quiet. She did as she was told. We all sat fearful on the couch, listening to the woman get her ass beat. She was hollering and screaming so loudly that Karrine had shielded her ears too. She started to cry. That was when I reached for her face and squeezed her chubby cheeks.

"Don't you start that crying, girl. Wipe those tears and get underneath the covers with Chyna. This will all be over with soon enough, okay?"

Karrine slowly nodded. She did as she was told. I held Simone closer to my chest, and with every loud thump coming from the bedroom, my body jumped. I wasn't sure if Ray was going to kill that woman. From the sound of it, it didn't appear that she was going to make it out alive.

"Heeeelp me," she cried out. "Somebody . . . anybody, please heeeelp! This Negro lost his everlasting miiiiiind!"

There was a loud boom. I predicted that Ray had picked her up and slammed her, because after that, there was silence. Then there was whimpering. The bedroom door flew open, and Chyna and Karrine hurried to pull the covers over their heads. I hated for them to witness shit like this, and this was not the kind of place where I wanted any of us to live. The apartment was tiny as hell, and because of our trifling neighbors, we couldn't get rid of the roaches. Ray hadn't given me one single dime for furniture and all we had was hand-me-downs from the Goodwill. Most of the time, my babies slept on the same plaid couch that made our skin itch. And the dingy white walls made me feel like the place was caving in on me day by day.

I heard another loud noise then watched as Ray tossed the woman out of the bedroom like she was a dirty ragdoll. She skidded on the wooden floor, probably catching splinters in her legs and hands like I had done when he knocked me on my ass. Her whole face was bloody and bruised, and her hair was wet and matted to her head. With a busted lip, she looked up at me with fiery red eyes.

"Wo . . . would you please, please help me? For God's sake, I need your hellllp."

She extended her trembling hand to me while holding her wounded side. I could tell she was in a lot of pain, but I looked away and didn't say shit. Ray dared me to.

"If you get off that couch, I'ma get yo' ass too. Stay there or else."

He wrapped the woman's long hair in his hand and started dragging her across the floor. Her legs flopped around like a dying fish as she kicked and screamed, begged and pleaded for Ray to let her go.

"I'ma let you go right now. And don't you ever bring yo' ass back here again!"

Ray opened the door and pushed the woman out of it. Seconds later, I could hear her tumbling down the stairs. Been there, done that too. He slammed the door and rushed back into the living room with a heaving chest. His muscle-packed, dark-skinned body dripped with beads of sweat. His dick was hanging, and he didn't have on one stich of clothing.

"Hurry up and put that girl to sleep. Meet me in the apartment across the hall. I want some pussy. And you'd better make that shit good, because that bitch left me high and dry."

High and dry, yet his dick was crusty from her wetness. I swear this was pure torture. After he done had his dick pushed up inside of that bitch, that nigga wanted to stuff it in me. That didn't work for me but, like always, I kept my mouth shut.

Ray went to the kitchen to get some water. When he came back, he stood by the couch, eyeballing me. I could tell he wanted to fight, but he couldn't think of a reason to get into my shit. As I paid him no attention, his eyes shifted to Chyna. He licked around his lips and touched his manhood. I spoke up, just to direct his attention elsewhere.

"The girls shouldn't really see you like that, Ray. Ain't you gon' go put some clothes on?" I said.

He ignored me. The way he looked at Chyna made my heart skip a beat. It made me real nervous. And while I didn't want to go into the apartment across the hall to fuck his ass, I figured that he would find other options if I didn't. He rolled his eyes and slammed the door on his way out.

At that moment, I laid Simone on the couch and turned to Chyna. Her beautiful, big, watered-down eyes stared at me. I could tell she was frightened.

"You don't have to be afraid of him," I said to her. "But, please tell me, has he ever touched you? Has he ever put his hands on you and touched you in an inappropriate place?"

Chyna blinked and hesitated to answer. She then lowered her head and slowly moved her head from side to side. "No," she said softly.

I lifted her chin and made her look me in the eyes. "Are you sure? You wouldn't lie to me, would you, Chyna?"

"No."

"Are you sure?"

She nodded and blinked tears from her eyes.

I wasn't sure if she had told me the truth. Something didn't seem right with her. Something didn't add up, but after I begged her to tell me the truth, she insisted the truth was no. Still, I didn't believe her.

With that in mind, shit was about to change. This was my turning point. I had to come up with a plan. My motto: "don't know no love, don't show no love," especially to a no-good motherfucking nigga who I suspected was a child molester. That's how I now viewed Ray. While I believed Chyna refused to tell me the truth, a mother knows. We fucking know when a nigga has definitely crossed the line with our daughters. I hoped like hell that I was wrong, though, and I kept telling myself that there was a possibility that I was wrong.

I gave Simone to Chyna and asked her to keep an eye on her sister for a while. While Ray was across the hall waiting for me, I went into the kitchen. My head still hurt from when he'd pulled my hair. My full lips were dry and my thick, natural hair was scattered all over my head. I snatched open the kitchen drawer and saw my reflection in a sharp, shiny knife that I intended to cut Ray with. I quickly removed it from the drawer and held it in my hand. With my dingy nightgown on, I marched across the hallway and into the other apartment where Ray was.

The other apartment was used for so-called business. It was where Ray handled most of his drug transactions and packaged his goods. On occasion, he brought his tricks there to fuck them, and he stashed a lot of money there, too. It was also where he spent some of his time with his eleven-year-old son, Honey. He was a good kid. He was nothing like Ray, but Ray always wanted him to live separate from the girls. He never wanted them to meet each other, and the girls knew nothing of their stepbrother, who had been working for Ray for as long as I could remember.

It was a good thing that Honey spent most of his time living with his grandmother, though. But, whenever he was around Ray, Ray taught him how to live dirty. How to cheat people, how to package dope, and even how to kill. I had no say-so whatsoever, and there was little that I could do to protect Honey from the madman he'd known as his father.

While standing at the bedroom door, I sucked in a deep breath. I flung the door open, only to see Ray sitting on the bed next to Honey. He understood what a lowdown, dirty nigga his father was. And, deep down, I didn't believe that Honey really cared much for Ray. But, like all of us, he put up with Ray because he paid the bills, and he kicked out Honey a little something on the side for his hard work.

Ray looked at the knife in my hand and laughed. A joint was squeezed between his fingers. He took a hit then passed it to Honey. "Go ahead and take a puff from that muthafucka while I take care of this dumb bitch."

Honey sucked in heat from the joint and watched as Ray approached me. "Please don't hurt him," Honey said, gazing at the knife. "Is that why you got that knife in yo' hand?"

My intentions were to cause some serious damage to Ray, but I couldn't do that shit in front of Honey. I refused to cut that fool up into a thousand pieces right in front of his son and have him live with that shit for the rest of his life. Honey meant too much to me. Even though he wasn't my child, I still had mad love for him.

"You heard him," Ray said, standing in front of me. "What you plannin' to do with that knife? Use it?"

He now had on a pair of jeans and socks. His hands were bruised from beating the white woman so bad, and there were several long scratches on the side of his face. At least she'd gotten something out of the deal.

"I . . . I came over here to see if you wanted something to eat. I was about to cut up some chicken and fry it," I lied.

Ray's eyes narrowed. Of course he didn't believe me. "I just beat one bitch's ass. Now you gon' make me go there again. I told you I wanted some pussy, didn't I? If I told you that, why in the fuck are you over here talkin' about chicken? Put the damn knife down and take off yo' clothes."

As soon as Ray said that, Honey blinked and nervously sucked in more heat from the joint. I laid the knife on the dresser and, as I was told, I removed my nightgown. Ray pushed me on the king-sized bed. Honey jumped up, moving away from us. He looked at his father, who smiled at him while darting his finger at me.

"I'ma teach you how to be a man," Ray said to Honey. "The first thing you need to know is all a bitch is good for is havin' babies and lyin' on her back. You don't need her for shit else, and don't believe the hype about cookin'. Many of these bitches should be banned from cookin', so learn to cook for yo'self. Love shouldn't be a part of your playbook, and the only muthafucka you need to love is yo'self. You hear me?"

Honey slowly nodded. He looked at me lying naked on the bed with sympathy in his young eyes. I didn't think Ray would be stupid enough to have sex with me in front of his son, but I guess I gave him too much credit. Today, though, what he wanted was his dick sucked. I guess he'd changed his mind about the pussy.

He laid one foot on the bed and made me sit up. I barely got a chance to open my mouth, before he rammed his dick into my mouth and shoved it deep down my throat. Rammed it so hard that I felt vomit creeping up my throat and choked. I swallowed so it would go back down. Tears filled my eyes, and as Ray held a tight grip on my hair, continuing with his madness, Honey looked on.

"See, this is how you do it," Ray said. "Make her give you pleasure. Every man should have a woman who's a good dick sucker. If you don't hook up with one, make sure you move on to the next. This one right here," he said, referring to me, "she's fine, got a bad-ass body and smooth chocolate skin. Got thick, natural hair, sexy light brown eyes, and on a scale from one to ten, I give her a twenty. I got beautiful babies by this bitch, but bein' fine don't mean shit. What really counts is the pussy. She got finger-lickin' good pussy and she gives decent head. Once she gets done doin' me, I'ma let her slob on yo' shit so you can see what's up."

My eyes widened. I slowed my mouth action. That was when Ray slapped his hand across my head and demanded that I continue. I swear this day was one of those days I wanted to push to the back of my mind and try to forget. Thing was, I couldn't forget. I suspected that Ray had been doing something to my child, he fucked another woman in my bed, and now he wanted me to suck his son's dick. There was no way in hell that was going to happen. It was obvious that Ray had been watching too much Danny Glover in *The Color Purple*. And even though many old-school niggas wanted control over their women like this, I assumed that they weren't trying to get their women to make men out of their sons by giving them blowjobs.

My mind raced. I had to do something. Something to stop Ray today and let him know that I wasn't as foolish as he thought I was. He didn't believe that I was capable of doing anything to him. He saw me as weak. True to the fact or not, everyone can be pushed. I had reached my limit.

Ray's dick was dripping with my saliva. His head was dropped back, eyes were closed and mouth was wide open. His loud moans echoed throughout the room. He continued to thrust fast into my mouth, damn near knocking out my teeth. I could see Honey from the corner of my eye. His eyes were without a blink. It looked as if his breathing had halted, and a slow tear rolled from the corner of his eye. It pained me to see him so hurt. It pained me to see all of the kids hurt by this, but I didn't have the power. With money came power. I had no money, no job, no nothing. That put Ray in a position to control me and do as he wished.

I waited until Ray's legs started to weaken. It wasn't long before they did. At this point, I could hear Honey sniffling. I guessed he figured I would be forced to get on my knees and do him next.

"What the fuck you over there whimperin' for? Grow the fuck up and be my li'l man," Ray said to Honey. "You ain't got no idea how this shit feels, but you gon' learn today how guuuud this bitch is to me. Trust, she gon' be good to you too. Tighten those jaws and move faster. Go faster!"

I had a headache and couldn't go any faster. I didn't have to because the second Ray released a drop of semen into my mouth, I chomped down on his dick like I was a pit bull. Bit into it so hard that I could taste his blood stirring in my mouth. Some of his skin rested on my teeth. He screamed so loudly that my ears rang. I hurried to back away from him, as he cupped his dick and crashed to his knees.

"Ahhhhhhhhhhhhhhhhh, daaaaaaaaaamn," he hollered out in pain. He could barely catch his breath. I scrambled to get the fuck out of there and slipped on my ass, right at the front door. Still, Ray couldn't catch me. He was in too much pain. I rushed into the other apartment and hurried to get my girls.

"Where are we going, Mama?" Karrine asked, rubbing her sleepy eyes.

"Out. We're getting the fuck out of here, now! Hurry!"

Five minutes later, we were out and in one of Ray's cars that I had stolen. We had no place to go, no one to turn to, no nothing. The shelter was full, and when I tried to explain my situation to a Caucasian woman who was supposed to be in charge, she stared at me as if I was the most pathetic bitch she had ever seen.

"How long did you say this has been going on?" she asked. I could tell she didn't care. Her demeanor said so. All she was there for was a paycheck.

"For too long. Can you help me? Please help me. I have no place to go, and we haven't had anything to eat all day."

"If I could help, I would. But as I said to you before, our facility is full. We get mothers like you coming in here all the time. And while we can help some, there is no way for us to help all. You've got to figure out a way to help yourself and stop having all these babies, especially if you don't have the means to take care of them. It's really not our responsibility to take care of them, so maybe you should go back home and see if you and the kids' father can work something out."

See, it was shit like this that made me crazy. Shit like this that made me never want to reach out to a motherfucker again for help. All her words did was give me a reason to never bring my ass back here again. I left, and for the next two days, me and my babies basically lived out of the car and ate leftovers from trashcans. It wasn't long before I had to take my ass back to that nigga Ray and apologize.

Chapter Two

I hated to go crawling back to Ray but, for now, I didn't have a choice. It took some shit like this to happen in order for me to realize what a messed-up situation I had put myself in. For so many years, I didn't realize how badly I'd handicapped myself. Ray had been ten steps, twenty steps, ahead of the game, and I was left far behind.

The one thing I was sure of was that I couldn't change everything overnight. Shit took planning. It required me to be sneaky and bring into the fold someone I could straight-up trust. The only person I could trust was Honey. But he was just a kid. He was still in school, and his bitch-ass grandmother, Selena, she hated me. She hated that Honey and I had gotten close. Instead of blaming Ray's no-good ass for Honey's problems, she blamed me.

With that being said, I had to be careful. This time, Ray already told me that after one more fuckup from me, I was going to be dead and the girls would be sent to a foster care home. I believed every word that nigga spewed. He sat at the kitchen table, chastising me and telling me what I needed to do going forward in order to make things right.

"One more time, bitch, and yo' ass is history. I don't give a fuck about you or them girls for real, and I'd be surprised if any of those bitches belonged to me. My dick been out of order since you bit it. I'm tired of kickin' yo' ass, and the one I gave you last night should've knocked some sense into you."

He's damn right it did. It knocked more sense into me than it had ever done before. Truthfully, I'd become numb from Ray's ass kickings. It never did me much good to holler and scream because no one ever came to the rescue. However, last night was the first time I attempted to fight back. It surprised me that Ray backed off a bit. Still, it left me with a black eye, a swollen lip, and bruises on my arms and legs. It was no secret that I was a battered woman, with no place to go, no friends whatsoever, and no damn self-esteem. Unfortunately, nobody ever told me that niggas like Ray existed. I thought that when a man told you that he loved you, he really meant that shit. I had to learn about men from scratch and, day by day, I learned how foul some of these niggas can be.

"And since I'm tired of kickin' yo' ass," Ray said, massaging his ashy hands together, "I have somethin' better that I want you to do. Tonight, you gon' make me some straight-up dough. There ain't no need for you to be sittin' on all that good pussy and not puttin' it to use."

I swallowed hard and wondered what exactly Ray was talking about. He didn't explain anything to me, but when eight o'clock rolled around, Ray ordered me to put on some clothes. I had been feeding Simone and was watching TV with the girls.

"Put on some clothes for what?" I challenged. "I was in the middle of something, Ray."

"Just do like I told you to do and stop givin' me so much mouth. Pass that bitch to her sisters and let Chyna or Karrine feed her. You and me got some work to do. Work that may take all night."

I had been called a bitch so much that I started to change my name on my birth certificate. I hesitated to move for a few minutes, but in order to keep the peace tonight, I gave Simone to Chyna.

"See about her for me, okay? Don't stay up late watching TV, and I'll be back as soon as I can."

The sadness in my girls' eyes tore at my soul. Their young minds couldn't process all that was going on, but I knew they could tell that something wasn't right. I felt horrible about it all. I knew I was failing my daughters. If I didn't get us out of this fucked-up situation soon, they would grow up to be passive just like me, or they would be without me. One or the other.

As Ray and I rode quietly in the car together, I was now positive of one thing. He didn't want a repeat of the other day. He knew what I was capable of doing to him, if he took me to that point again. To me, it seemed as if he had a little fear in him. He was reluctant to say anything to me, considering that when we used to ride in the car together, all I'd hear was his big mouth yelling and calling me names.

Today, there was silence. He looked straight ahead while tapping his fingers on the steering wheel. Music crooned in the background. His fancy black Cadillac with red crushed-velvet seats rolled down the highway next to cars that couldn't compare. Ray didn't allow me to ride with him that often, and the only car he'd let me use was a beat-up Mustang that had a loud, hanging muffler. It wasn't as if that was a big deal because Ray always gave me and my girls just enough to get by. If I cooked steak for him, we ate ham sandwiches. If he drank wine, we had water. The apartment across the hall looked ten times better than the one we lived in, and Ray didn't have to sleep and eat with roaches. We did. That's what happens when a nigga controls you. It's either his way, or no fucking way at all.

Ray pulled in front of a two-story brick home. There looked to be some type of party going on because numerous cars were parked out front. Music thumped loudly and several men were on the porch drinking. Ray grabbed a brown paper bag with vodka in it. He turned it up to his lips and guzzled it down. He took several hard swallows then passed the bag to me.

"Take a few swigs of this and straighten yo' hair. I like what you got on, but always remember that red is yo' color."

I drank from the bottle then laid it next to me. I didn't know my hair was out of place, and it shouldn't have been because I'd sprayed so much hairspray on it. My hair, however, was too thick. It was tinted with blond streaks and fell several inches past my shoulders. The feathery part almost covered my left eye, so I moved it away from my face and painted my lips with more red gloss. My makeup was on heavy because I needed to hide my bruises. And dressed in a black stretch dress that rested on my curves, I felt as if it was sexy enough. The V-dip in the front almost met up with my navel, and a sliver of my small breasts peeked out.

"Done," I said, looking over at Ray. "Now what?"

"Now, you go inside with me and you don't speak unless you're spoken to. You don't pay any of these niggas extra attention and you do as I tell you to do. After you're done, you come back to the car and wait on me."

There was a little snap in my voice when I asked Ray another question. "I mean, what exactly am I supposed to be doing? I don't get it."

Ray reached over and grabbed my hair from the back. He yanked my head and pulled it back so far that I thought he was about to break my fucking neck. "You've reached your limit today, so you don't get to ask me any more questions. All you need to do is what I tell you. Got it?"

I tried to nod, but couldn't even do that. Ray released my head by shoving it forward. I rolled my eyes and turned my head to look out the window.

"You've been gettin' real bold these days," he said. "Watch yourself, girl. Watch it."

Ray sprayed several dashes of perfume in my cleavage and laughed when he sprayed a dash between my legs. He screwed the cap on the perfume bottle and told me to put it in my purse.

"Let's go. Keep a smile on that pretty face and let these muthafuckas know that you proud to be Ray McWilliams's bitch."

He opened the car door then walked to my side of the car and opened the door for me. He damn sure didn't have good manners, and all of this was one big front.

As Ray strutted up the steps and approached some of his friends, they all looked on to check him out. I could see hate as well as jealousy locked in their eyes. Again, Ray wasn't a bad-looking nigga. He was dark skinned, had a shapely afro, and he wore a trimmed goatee. The fur coat he had draped on his shoulders made him look like a million bucks. I wasn't sure how much money he had, but with all the drug selling he'd been doing for years, I knew he had plenty. But there was no fun in being a dopeman's sidekick, having his children, and being abused and broke.

Ray greeted his friends, but didn't introduce me to any of them. Many of their eyes were filled with lust, but I did what I was told to do: I smiled and kept it moving. As we made our way inside, the crib was thick with nothing but niggas. I could tell there was some kind of birthday celebration going on, because HAPPY BIRTHDAY banners were draped from one doorway to the next. A sheet cake was on the table in the living room and balloons were propped up in several places as well. A gang of alcohol was being passed around, and there was a bartender who was serving it up in a big way. While Ray hung our coats, he told me to go get us something to drink.

"What do you want to drink?" I said with an attitude. I damn sure didn't want to be in a house filled with musty, loud-talking, drunk-ass men.

"How you gon' stand there and ask me what I want to drink? You supposed to be my woman. Therefore, you should already know what I drink without askin'."

"Then I guess I'll order up you some piss then, because I really don't pay attention to what you drink."

Ray's eyes cut me like a sharpened knife. I knew I was out of line, but I had started to push back, even if it was just a little. "Order up some piss, and I'ma order up a fist to yo' fuckin' face. Get the hell away from me and go find somethin' else to do until I need you."

I rolled my eyes and walked away. As I made my way through the crowds of men, they parted and watched my every move. Some spoke, some didn't. Some smiled, some frowned. I figured that many of them didn't know who I was, but I had seen some of them before. Particularly at Ray's apartment, buying dope or helping him package it.

"What's up, TD?" Miles said, touching my hand. Miles was one of Ray's closest friends. He wasn't as bad as Ray was, and I appreciated that he was always kind to me.

"Hello, Miles," I stopped to say. "What brings you to a crappy party like this?"

Miles lifted his glass, which contained brown liquid and ice. "She goes by the name of free Hennessy, all night. This bitch manages to hook me every single time. And I damn sure ain't gon' pass up good food. They done hooked this shit up for Lorenzo's birthday, and that nigga ain't even here yet."

I laughed and didn't say much else to Miles because Ray was side-eying me from afar. Instead, I walked up to the bartender and asked for vodka, no ice, and Hennessy. He quickly made the drinks, and I moseyed on back to where Ray was sitting on a leather sectional with about nine or ten other men. Mountains of cocaine were on the table, with blunts and more alcohol. There were also stacks of dollar bills on the table, along with a lot of change.

I handed Ray the glass of Hennessy and he thanked me. He pulled me by the waist, making me sit on his lap.

"For those of y'all who don't already know, this right here is my bitch, TD. She bad, ain't she?"

I guessed I was supposed to smile, but my expression remained flat. His "bitch" references never sat well with me, and the only reason he called me TD was because he didn't want any of his friends to know my real name. He never wanted anyone to know nothing about me. That's why it surprised me that he'd asked me to come to this party with him tonight.

"Hell, yeah, she bad," one man said, swiping white powder from his nose. "One of the finest bitches I done ever laid my eyes on. Say, sugga. You got any sisters, cousins, or nieces? I got plenty of dough, and they wouldn't have to do nothin' at all but cook and fuck me."

The men laughed and slammed their hands against each other. All I did was shrug, until I felt Ray nudge me with his elbow.

"The man asked you a question," he said. "What, you can't talk? Cat got your tongue or does a dog have it? I mean, bitch, say somethin'."

The fool told me to keep my mouth shut, but since I could now speak, I said what was on my mind. "No, I don't have any sisters. I don't have any friends, cousins, or nieces. If I did, they wouldn't be interested in any of Ray's friends, who only want them to cook for them and fuck them. Personally, I think a woman can find something else better to do with her time."

Silence fell over the entire room and all eyes were on me. The man's eyes grew wide and the rest of them appeared taken aback by my words.

"Man, you'd better get yo' bitch. She got a slick mouth that needs to be dealt with."

Embarrassed as hell, Ray jumped up and knocked me off his lap. I stumbled, but didn't fall. He ordered me into the bathroom, where he slammed the door and rushed up to me. He gripped my face with his hands, squeezing it as tightly as he could. My head was pushed against the wall and he held it steady so I couldn't move.

"What in the fuck is wrong with you? Didn't I give you orders before we came in here? Consider this yo' warnin'. If you don't get yo' shit together, I'ma drill my foot in yo' ass, right in front of everybody. So think again before you open yo' mouth and act."

Ray gave me a smack across my head then shoved me toward the mirror. "Straighten yo'self up. Then come on out here and do yo' thing. I'ma need for you to shake that ass tonight and make us some money. It's the least you can do for damn near bitin' my dick off and embarrassin' me."

"You mean, shake my ass, as in stripping?" I questioned.

"I mean, shake yo' ass as in dancin' to the music, teasin' the men out there, bendin' over, and lookin' sexy as shit. You can constitute that as strippin' if you want to, and as a matter of fact, showin' some of that big ass you got might not be a bad thing. The more ass, the more money."

I suspected that Ray was up to something like this. It had definitely crossed my mind. But he knew damn well that this wasn't about "us" making money. It was about me making money and giving it to him. I sure as hell wondered what he would do if I said no. Since I was in the mood to fuck with him, I went for it.

"Ray, I had no idea that taking my clothes off and shaking my ass for your posse is what you wanted me to do. I am the mother of your children, you know? Don't you have any respect for me? How or why would you want me to put myself out there, and the truth is, I don't think I can do it."

He sucked his teeth and stepped forward. His eye twitched. I could tell that I was getting underneath his skin.

"You can do it and you will. And you want me to tell you why? Because my dick ain't been able to get hard since you did what you did with those sharp-ass teeth of yours. I ain't been pissin' right and my shit still hurts when I think about it. This is called consequences. Either do as I say or get the fuck out of my place."

I just stood there, staring at him. He knew exactly what to say to me, and for a person who didn't have no place to turn right now, there really was no other option. No fucking options, and I laughed to myself at people who judged me and thought that there was a system in place to help my black ass and my babies out of this situation. Back then, people were sadly mistaken. Now, things are different, but at the moment, I was in this shit by myself.

But instead of looking at it from a negative angle, I thought of a way to use this to my advantage. The way to fuck with a nigga as ignorant as Ray was to get at him through his friends.

Ray left the bathroom, but not before telling me to bring my A-game with me. While I had never done anything so ridiculous, the truth was I could dance and I knew how to be and look sexy. That's what attracted Ray to me in the beginning.

I left the bathroom and walked through a cloud of thick smoke. Lorenzo had finally arrived and many of the others greeted him. I was pleased to see another woman in the house. I wondered if she was asked to do the same thing as me. Then again, by the way she was dressed, I doubted it. She rocked a one-piece, blue jean jumpsuit with a belt that tightened at her waist. Unlike me, she was very friendly with the other men.

"Shirley, come on over here and have a seat," Ray said. "I told Lorenzo that I'ma steal you from him."

Shirley blushed and sauntered her way over to Ray. I could always tell when Ray had fucked another woman before, and trust me when I say he and Shirley had definitely been there, done that before. Lorenzo looked kind of taken aback by the way Shirley was all over Ray. He fake smiled at them, and then he went to the bar to get something to drink. Afterward, someone cranked up the music. Ray stood and spoke loudly over the music as he asked for everyone to give him their attention. Many of the niggas did, but some continued talking and laughing at Joe, who was a wannabe comedian. He kept telling jokes while Ray was trying to make an announcement.

"Joe, shut yo' fat ass up until I get done talkin'."

Joe looked embarrassed as hell, but he didn't dare say anything back to Ray. Like many of the niggas in here knew, saying the wrong thing to Ray had dire consequences.

"As I was sayin' before that muthafucka rudely interrupted me, I got a surprise for y'all tonight. All I ask is that y'all show her a li'l appreciation for her time, and send her home with a big smile on her face. Niggas, I give y'all my bitch. Y'all always talking about how y'all would love to get freaky with my woman, so here she is. Touch, but don't get too carried away. 'Cause no matter how hard y'all dicks may get, the only dick that she'll be gettin' tonight will be mine."

The men laughed and many heads turned in my direction. I stood near a corner with my arms folded. While I was definitely nervous, I did my best not to let it show. A blank expression was locked on my face, and I held back the tears that I wanted so badly to fall. After all, crying wasn't going to save me.

The volume of the music went up several notches and as a new joint spilled through the speakers, it was my time to shine. I swallowed the oversized lump in my throat and boldly strutted through the men who had all gathered around in one big circle. The floor cleared for me to do my thing, and my head was held up high. I shifted my eyes to Ray who was sitting next to Shirley with his arm around her shoulder. With that, I made it my business not to look at him again. *Disrespectful bastard.*

"Show us what ya workin' wit', TD," one man said. "With all that ass you got, I know it shouldn't be a problem."

I couldn't help but to take another peek at Ray again. He nodded then tossed back the drink in his hand. He slowly winked at me then nodded again.

Before I knew it, I started moving my body around like a slithering snake. My hands roamed my curves and I began to feel all over myself. I ran my fingers through my hair, making it messy. I focused in on two men in particular: Lorenzo and Miles. I batted my eyelashes and shot them seductive looks that immediately drew them into my performance. They were definitely tuned in, especially when I lowered one shoulder of my dress and showed my chocolate skin. I could see some of the other men licking their lips with their breath held. They had no idea where I was going to venture to, but as Ray had requested, I intended to go all out.

After I dropped the other shoulder of my dress, I lowered it underneath my breasts. They stood at attention, firm as ever. Every single eye in the room was on me and many of the niggas stood frozen in time. That was, with the exception of one. He walked up to me and eased a twenty dollar bill inside of my panties. He also took a swipe at my breasts and smiled.

"You are finer than red wine, baby," he whispered. "Ray is one lucky man."

I was glad he thought so. And even though that was supposed to be a compliment, I had no reason to smile. There was seriousness trapped in my eyes that I wouldn't break for nothing. And no matter how much money these niggas dropped on me tonight, I felt used and disgusted. Still, I had turned my thoughts elsewhere and tried my best to make the best of this situation.

Minutes later, I stood in nothing but my silk black panties that rested high on my hips and showed off my curves. Dollars were tucked inside of my panties, and more money was scattered on the floor around me. I was bent over, exposing my hairless slit to the niggas who stood behind me. I could hear their moans and groans when I moved the crotch section aside and dipped my long finger inside of me.

"Fuck this shit," one man said. "My dick so damn hard, I can't take it. All I want to do is bust that shit wide open right now!"

The man next to him slammed his hand against his. "I need to taste that sweet mutha. It looks sweet as a sweet potato pie. Ray, what it tastes like, man? I need to know!"

Ray sat there looking as if he was the prize-winner. With all of the money scattered on the floor, of course he was. "Nigga, you ain't got enough money to taste it. Ain't none of y'all got enough money to taste it, so don't get your hopes up."

"Well, if I can't taste it, I'm damn sure gon' touch it."

The man waved a hundred dollar bill in the air, showing it to Ray. Everybody looked on as he came up to me and rubbed his hands on my ass. He squeezed it a few times, but there wasn't no chance in hell that I was going to allow him to touch inside of me. I removed the hundred dollars from his hand and placed it between my lips. As I stared him down, I inched forward and pressed my breasts against his chest. I slithered my body against his, and when I turned around, I bounced my ass against him. I could feel his hardness poking me. The muthafucka felt way bigger than Ray's, and I'd be the first to admit that his dick wasn't about nothing.

As the man behind me talked shit and rubbed my ass, so did the others. At ten dollars a pop, Ray invited them to do as they wished, with the exception of sticking their dicks inside of me or using their fingers. I was eaten up inside. I could have gotten a damn bat and beat the shit out of these hungry, thirsty niggas who probably had bitches at home in bed waiting for them. But there they were groping me. Feeling me up, as if I were the last woman on earth.

At this point, I was so angry that I ignored Ray altogether. My eyes stayed locked on Miles, who I could tell didn't approve of this. He appeared to have sympathy for me. He looked as if he wanted to come rescue me. Then again, maybe his eyes were saying how badly he wanted to fuck me. If that were the case, I was in business. Fucking Miles would eat Ray alive, simply because they were competitors more than they were friends. I wanted Ray to see my eyes locked on Miles. It was all in my plan tonight, but for now, I had to get through this madness.

"I ain't ever laid my eyes on an ass this round and pretty," one nigga said. He wiped across his wet, juicy lips and planted a kiss on my right ass cheek. "I'ma need to get the hell out of here and settle this dick of mine down. Ray, this bitch is bad. My ass gon' have a heart attack."

Ray didn't respond, and I didn't dare look his way. My eyes remained on Miles. I figured that Ray would notice, and after a while, he surely did. As I stood grinding my body against another man, Ray jumped in front of me.

"That's enough," he shouted. "Now, y'all niggas done had y'all selves a good time tonight with my woman. She lookin' wore out, so back away from her and let's finish partyin'."

Finally, I spoke up. "I'm not tired, Ray. Actually, I was kind of enjoying myself. Leave these niggas alone. They're just having fun."

Ray's eyes narrowed as he looked at me. The fools around me were very happy that I wasn't ready to call it quits. One even had his hand on my breast, massaging it.

Ray smacked his hand away and winced at me. "I said you're done. Get yo' clothes back on and go sit yo' ass in the car and wait for me."

Inside I was kind of smiling. On the outside, my expression didn't change. I swiped up my dress and threw it over my shoulder. As I made my way to the bathroom, several men smacked my ass and continued to touch me with their grimy hands. More money was dropped at my feet, but Ray ordered that trick Shirley to pick it all up.

I went into the bathroom and closed the door. Right then, I released a deep sigh and allowed some tears to fall. I wanted to shower so badly. I couldn't wait to get home to do so. That's all I wanted, along with a bed that I would, hopefully, sleep in alone tonight.

After I cleaned myself up in the bathroom, and put my dress back on, I walked out the door. Miles stood right outside of the door waiting for me.

"You got a minute?" he said.

My eyes shifted toward the living room area. I figured Ray would be looking for me, or that he would make sure I'd gone to the car as I was told.

"Don't worry about him," Miles said. "He's drunk as hell, and as you know, he's being entertained by someone else."

I guess Miles thought that would hurt my feelings, but it didn't. I was about to shrug, but I caught myself. Instead, I moved away from the door and followed Miles outside. We stood close to the house, smoking a blunt and talking.

"I don't know what's up with Ray, and if I could apologize for what that nigga has put you through, I would."

"Nobody can apologize for Ray but him. And at this point, an apology is not what I need from him."

Miles took a hit from the joint then swallowed the smoke. He pulled his leather jacket back and stared at me with lust in his hazelnut addictive eyes. I couldn't stand to look into them, so I lowered my head to gaze at the ground. Miles lifted my chin and made me look at him.

"Then what is it that you need? Tell me, TD. I promise not to say a word to Ray about this."

I wasn't sure if I could trust Miles. As I said before, the only person I trusted was Honey. He'd been my little soldier. I truly felt like he was really in my corner.

I swallowed and did my best not to show weakness. "What I need is my freedom. I want to get away from Ray and find an affordable place for me and my children. I want to never see his face again, and I also need some serious money. I'm broke. I don't have shit to call my own and this is not how I want the rest of my life to be."

Miles nodded as I spoke. I couldn't read him at all, but he came across as being sincere. "Your freedom? All you have to do is walk away. After that, why don't you come see me? I'll help you take care of that money problem, but you may have to be willin' to give me somethin' in return, too. As for not seein' Ray again, are you sayin' that you want him dead?"

I hesitated, but told the truth. "Yes, I do. I know he's your friend, but I hate him, Miles. You just don't know all that he's done to me. I'm telling you that you have no idea what he's capable of."

"Trust me, I do. But, I'll tell you what, maybe I can help you with that little problem, too. Who knows? There could be a chance that we can all get some of the little things that we want."

I stared into Miles's eyes and didn't hesitate to ask. "What do you want? I know you're not as eager to get rid of Ray as I am, are you?"

Miles shrugged his shoulders. "Maybe, but we'll talk about that at another time. As for what I want, let me show you what that is."

Miles flicked the joint in the grass and leaned in closer to me. He pressed his lips against mine, and then forced his tongue into my mouth. At first, I didn't reciprocate. But the more I'd thought about it, why not? This was the opportunity I had been waiting for. I could be free of Ray, and also make that nigga's head spin by fucking with his friend. But Miles was definitely no friend. He proved that when he lifted my dress and stretched my panties to my ankles. I stepped out of them and assisted him with lowering his jeans. They gathered at his ankles, along with his boxers. It wasn't long before he hiked me up to his waist and started grinding. My pussy locked on him like it had been there before. I had to admit that his dick felt much better than Ray's, and I loved the way Miles turned circles in my pussy and made it glaze his entire shaft. Without saying one word, I held on tight to his neck, as he pounded my insides and gave me the sexual pleasure I so desperately needed.

"It feels good, doesn't it?" he boasted. "And just for the record, this shit you got feels good too."

All I did was nod. My back was against the wall, and with my legs straddled wide, while Miles held me up, I enjoyed every bit of it. I had been faking orgasms with Ray, but I could feel the one that was about to come. It started at the very tips of my curled toes. My legs trembled and my body got weak. Miles sped up his pace, and before I knew it, we both did an exchange of fluids. We were out of breath and couldn't stop gazing into each other's eyes.

"I hope to give you much more of that," Miles said. "For now, go chill in the car and wait for Ray. We'll talk tomorrow. I think you may be pleased about what I offer you and your girls."

I couldn't lie. Hearing that shit pleased my heart. It made me smile. Maybe there was a way out of this, and if all Miles wanted was some good pussy, hell, I was all for it. He reached in his wallet and put several bills in my hand. I wasn't sure how much it was yet, but whatever it was, I was grateful. Especially since I figured that Ray wouldn't give me one single dime for my hard work tonight.

"Take that," Miles said. "You earned it, so go do something nice for yourself and the girls. Y'all deserve it."

I hurried to say, "Thanks." Maybe I wouldn't have to go through the trouble of involving Honey in my mess. The other day, I'd talked to him about how he could help me. Since he'd had access to Ray's apartment, I asked Honey to do some things that could get him in serious trouble. While he was reluctant to do it, he still agreed to help me. Maybe now, I wouldn't have to go that route and come between him and Ray's relationship.

Miles kissed my cheek and told me to go. With a dripping wet pussy, I rushed to the car and shut the door when I got inside. I opened my hand to see how much money Miles had given to me. It was five one-hundred-dollar bills. That made me smile again. It made me have just a little hope for me and my girls. Hope that I hadn't had in a very long time.

Chapter Three

Nearly an hour later, I saw Ray coming to the car. I had dozed off a few times, and I couldn't stop thinking about what my girls had been up to. Chyna was always looking out for her sisters. She was the oldest and she kept good care of them while I was away. But the truth was, she was just a kid herself. This was a lot on her, and I regretted that my problems had been pushed off on her.

I saw Ray give Shirley a kiss and then he walked away. He opened the car door and hopped in with a smirk on his face. As he looked over at me, he touched my chin.

"You did good," he said with a glassy film covering his eyes. "Better than I thought you would do, so from now on, this gon' be yo' new gig. I figured you had that shit in you. Those niggas in there loved it. If they paid like this, ain't no tellin' how much more money others niggas will pay."

Ray showed me the roll of money that he could barely grip his hand around. He shook it near my face then brought it up to his nose and sniffed it.

"This is what a bad bitch can do. I know you're upset with me, but as you know, I don't give a fuck about yo' feelings. My only complaint is I saw some of those bruises on your thighs. I'ma stop kickin' that ass for a while and let those bruises heal. Ain't no need for me to mess up my moneymaker; and who knows? I may even get some other bitches to join us. I'll let you organize the shit for me and find bitches who you think can turn up the heat like you. What you got to say about that?"

This nigga was crazy. All I could do was shake my head and try my best not to say the wrong thing. "I'm not sure, Ray, but my only question is where is my money? You talked about 'us' making money and you haven't dropped one single dime in my lap yet."

Ray snapped his finger and turned up the music. "Forgive me for bein' so goddamn self-ish," he said. "Here you go, baby. Go buy yo'self somethin' nice."

I'll be damned if Ray didn't drop a fucking dollar in my lap. He laughed and rolled the steering wheel in circles to do a U-turn. After he blew the horn at a few niggas standing outside, he sped down the street, high as ever and drunk as hell. I wasn't sure if we'd make it home, but I can honestly say that I had never been so happy to see my raggedy-ass apartment. As soon as Ray parked, I shot inside to go see about my babies. It was almost two o'clock in the morning. Thankfully, when I got inside, they were sound asleep.

I sighed from relief and went into the bedroom. The first thing I wanted to do was shower, so I gathered my pajamas and a few towels. Ray came into the bedroom and plopped face down on the bed. He was on his way to sleep, until the phone rang. I was never allowed to answer the phone, so I watched as he crawled on the bed and reached for the phone on the nightstand.

"Speak," he said.

I figured that it was one of his partners calling about a late-night drug run, or possibly that bitch Shirley who was eager to get some dick in her tonight. I surely hoped that was the case, because I'd had my taste of something good tonight, and I was in no mood for Ray.

I closed the closet and was on my way out the door to go take a shower. That's when I felt something solid as a rock slam into the side of my face. Immediately, all I saw was darkness with flashes of white lights. My skull felt like it had been crushed and all I could feel was throbbing in my head. Tears seeped from the corner of my eyes and I hit the floor so hard that I was sure I had broken something. My eyes fluttered, and all I could see was a blurred vision of Ray standing over me, pointing his finger at me.

"You ain't nothin' but a goddamn slut," he yelled. "I know for a fact what that nigga Miles told me wasn't true, but he ain't the kind of nigga who would lie to me." Ray squatted to my level and looked me in the eyes. "Did you give that fool my pussy tonight? Even after I told you that that shit belonged to me, tell me you didn't go there, did you? In addition to that, is it true that you want yo' freedom and that you wished me dead? Did you give that nigga some pussy to kill me?"

The whole left side of my face was numb. When I tried to open my mouth, it hurt so badly. I couldn't believe this shit, and as I sat on the floor thinking about it, all I could think about was my new rule: trust no nigga! All of them muthafuckas had an agenda. I should've known better than to think Miles would help me. I suspected that the only thing I'd get out of it was a good fuck, and the fact that I was back to my original plan with Honey didn't make me feel good.

I held the side of my face and was unable to feel my hand. I thought Ray had hit me with something, but the only thing he'd hit me with was his fist. I still hadn't said one word. That angered him even more.

"I need some answers, damn it! Speak the fuck up and let me hear what you got to say about this shit! Yo' ass is out of control, and what's up with that nigga giving you some money?"

For now, I remained silent. Just glared at him with hatred trapped in my eyes, and that angered him even more. He continued to rant.

"You don't have to say shit because I already know what's up. And what I need to do is throw you out on yo' ass tonight. You don't deserve to be here, and no bitch should be allowed to get away with what you've done to me."

Ray was so good at threatening me, but this time, I knew he was serious. Still, I didn't respond. I allowed him to get whatever he wanted to off his chest, and I remained crouched down on the floor, trying to soothe my pain.

"If I die," he said, spraying my face with his spit, "bitch, what you gon' do? You know damn well that you ain't shit without me. I can't believe that this is the kind of appreciation I get from you!"

He lifted his foot and punted my midsection.
I curled up in a knot and did my best to shield
my face and the rest of my body from his brutal
attack.

"I will never touch yo' nasty ass again," he
yelled. "Never again, but if you think I'm gon'
allow you to be free, you'd better think again. Yo'
ass stayin' right here with me. You gon' continue
to make me all the money I need, and if or when I
get tired of you, I will let you know."

Ray stood and unzipped his pants. He pulled
out his stubby dick and shook it with his hand. I
thought he was going to order me to give him a
blowjob, but instead, he dropped his head back
in relief and started pissing. His piss flowed all
over me, especially on top of my head. My hair
fell flat and his liquids ran down my face. The
smell of his urine was awful, and as some of it
flowed into my eyes, it burned.

Needless to say, pissing on somebody was one
damn way to get them fired up. Catching Ray off
guard, I rushed off the floor and started wildly
swinging on his ass. Like a raging madwoman, I
pounded his back and head. This time, he was the
one crouched down. He tried to grab my waist, but
I was too fast for him. I realized that my hands
alone weren't enough, so I started picking up shit
and throwing it at him. I started with shoes and

then wound up with the lamp in my hand. He ducked but the base of the lamp still hit him. It was a good thing that he was drunk, because as he charged at me, he stumbled. I whacked him with one of the speakers from the stereo and then swung out a chair like it was a baseball bat. The chair cracked across his back and sent him flying into the wall.

"Goddamn it!" he shouted as he grabbed the curtain to break his fall. The rod broke and sent him crashing down to the floor. He sat there, eyeing me with a heaving chest. I too was out of breath, and I held the chair up high, ready to throw it at him again.

"Pu . . . put that damn chair down," Ray said, panting and waving his hand. "We . . . we'll talk about this shit tomorrow."

My arms were so weak that I dropped the chair on the floor. I could barely catch my breath as I stared at Ray in a lot of pain.

"I don't want to talk about it anymore. What's done is done. If you don't want to touch me ever again, I'm perfectly fine with that. But, nigga, don't you ever do that mess to me again. Piss belongs in a toilet, not on me."

I turned to leave the room. Ray's comment stopped me dead in my tracks. "Damn, bitch. It was only pee. You act like I sprayed yo' dumb ass with poison."

I cut my eyes at Ray and left the room. I wasn't sure what else was going to happen to me that night, but I was damn proud of myself for fighting back again.

By morning, Ray was still slumped over on the floor, next to the window. He'd used the curtain as a sheet to cover up and was knocked out. I was in the kitchen making toast for Karrine and Chyna to eat with their cereal. Simone was in my arms, but she was irritable and crying.

"What's wrong with her?" I asked Chyna. "Was she like this last night?"

Chyna moved her head from side to side. "No. She went to sleep early while Karrine and me watched TV."

I looked at Karrine. She was always the quiet one who didn't have much to say. She and Chyna were very close. It was obvious that they loved each other a lot. When Chyna went to the bathroom, I turned to Karrine for answers.

"If something was going on with Chyna," I said to Karrine, "would you tell me?"

She nodded and continued to look down at her cereal bowl.

"Has she ever mentioned anything to you about Ray touching her?"

Like Chyna, Karrine said no. Maybe I had been barking up the wrong tree, and even I had to admit that I had never seen Ray do anything to her. Still, there was something about the way he looked at her that bothered me.

Before Chyna came back into the kitchen, Ray walked in. He stood in the doorway with a pair of boxers on. His dick poked through the hole and was clearly visible. His shirt was off, and I couldn't believe when I saw that he'd had a black eye, compliments of me.

"I don't smell shit in here cookin', so what am I supposed to eat?" he said as if something was clogged in his throat.

The second Chyna walked back into the kitchen, the direction of Ray's eyes traveled to her ass. She sat at the table and didn't dare to look his way. His eyes shifted back to me.

"What would you like for me to cook you?" I asked.

"Yet again, I've been yo' man for almost ten fuckin' years. If you don't know what I like to eat by now, figure it the fuck out."

Ray left the kitchen, and for the next hour or so, he was at the other apartment. That gave me time to cook his breakfast and lay Simone down for a nap. I also watched TV with Chyna and Karrine for a little while. When Ray returned, he ate breakfast and then told me he had to go make some runs.

"My son won't be here until four or five o'clock. When he gets here, take yo' ass over there and check on him a few times. I asked him to package up some shit for me. I need to make sure he do what I told him to do. As for you," Ray said, and pointed to his black eye, "the money you will make me tonight will squash this. Be ready to go by seven, not a minute later."

Ray left. For the next few hours there was peace and quiet. I cleaned up as best as I could, and then made my way over to the other apartment to check on Honey. After I knocked on the door, he opened it. I walked inside and saw that he was doing exactly what Ray had asked him to do. He was packaging dope with plastic gloves on. There was a table filled with narcotics. Pills, weed, crack, small bottles of a clear substance: you name it, it was there. I always knew Ray was into some heavy shit, but this was ridiculous.

"Did Ray say when he was coming back?" Honey asked me. "I forgot what he told me to do with this."

Honey held in his hand one of the bottles filled with white liquid. I damn sure didn't have a clue what to do with it, if anything.

"Just leave it. I'm sure he'll let you know what to do with it later."

Honey nodded and got back to work. As I sat there watching him, I could tell he was perfecting the drug game. He focused real hard on cooking and packaging the drugs the right way. The seriousness in his eyes said that he didn't want to make any mistakes. I couldn't help but to think that, one day, he could be very beneficial to me. I had already spoken to him about stealing money from Ray, but now I had some other ideas as well.

I lit a cigarette and took several puffs from it. Honey looked at me from across the table and smiled.

"I got that for you," he said. "But you gotta promise me that you won't ever tell Ray. If you do, he gon' beat my ass, like he do yours. I don't ever want to catch a beat down like that, you know what I mean?"

"I know exactly what you mean. I wouldn't want him to ever hurt you like that either, but I hope you understand that I have to do what I must do to get myself out of this fucked-up situation. I hate putting you in the middle of my mess, but you're the only person I can trust right now, Honey. And trust me when I say that I owe you a lot for helping me."

"Naw, you don't owe me nothing. I just feel bad for you, that's all. I don't like how Ray treats you, and as my grandmother says, you deserve better."

"Your grandmother said that about me? Really?"

"Yep. She likes you a lot, and all she's ever said about you is that you are one dumb bitch for staying with Ray. She told me that if she were you, she'd set him on fire. I told her that I don't think you would do anything like that because you love him too much. Besides, I wouldn't let you do anything like that either. After all, he is my dad and he does take care of me."

It angered me that Honey's grandmother said that about me, and even though she was right, she just didn't understand my situation. Motherfuckers could always sit back and judge your situation, without walking one damn day in your shoes. Honey was so wrong about me loving Ray, though. There wasn't an ounce of love left for him in my body. I hated that nigga's guts. But I didn't want Honey to ever know how much I truly despised his father.

Honey walked away from the table and returned with a stash of money in his hand. He gave it to me. "Here. I don't know how much it is, but I tried to make sure he wouldn't notice it was missing. And you say you want me to go into his stash every week, right?"

"Yes. Every week, until I give you the word to stop. I'm going to put some of this aside for you, too, and the day will come when neither of us won't have anything to worry about."

Honey smiled and got back to business. "You may not have any worries, but I surely do," he said.

"Are you talking about Ray? Don't worry about him, okay? If he ever questions the money, I will tell him that I took it."

"I'm not worried about the money because there's too much of it in there. He won't notice that it's missing. I be getting me a little of it from time to time too." Honey giggled and so did I.

Smart kid. Very smart kid.

"Anyway, I was talking about my grandmother. She's real sick, you know? She got cancer and it's just a matter of time before she dies. I'm okay staying with Ray, but if something happens to her, I'm gon' be real miserable. I love my granny. She's always been like a mama to me."

I scooted in and wrapped my arms around Honey. "We will pray like hell that nothing happens to her, but if it does, please know that you always got me, okay? From this day forward, you can always count on me. In the meantime, I have some other ideas that I want to share. When all is said and done, we gon' be on top of the world. We both gon' be the boss, and Ray can take all of this shit over here and go to hell. Are you with me on this or not? If not, I understand."

Honey slapped his hand against mine and said that he was down for whatever. That day, and the days and weeks following, he proved to me just how loyal he really was.

Chapter Four

That nigga, Ray, had no idea what kind of woman he had created: a real bitch who was starting to live up to the title he'd given me. Eventually, I would become a pain in his ass and a force to be reckoned with. See, it took a nigga like Ray to turn a good girl into bad. I hadn't been feeling like myself, but that wasn't necessarily a bad thing. It had gotten to the point where Ray would walk off and leave me the fuck alone. I would say something smart to his ass, and he would let that shit ride. He continued with his threats, but for now, they went in one ear and out the other. I was starting to get my mojo. Honey had been dropping a lot of dough in my hands, and we'd planned something big that would finally set me free.

For now, though, I was back in the streets, shaking my ass and making that fool, Ray, all the money he could get his grimy hands on. I had to laugh to myself, because he seriously thought that I wasn't getting paid. He got a kick out of dropping those dollar bills into my lap at the end of the night, and he had the nerve to joke about it, saying that I was now up to twenty-five dollars.

I laughed that shit off too. All while putting the money that Honey kept giving me into the bank. I'd put his name on the account, too, just in case something happened to me and he needed access to it. We were a real team. He trusted everything that I said and did. Ray was too busy into what he'd been doing that he didn't even notice how close Honey and I had gotten.

I stood at the door in Ray's apartment, ready to go to my next gig. Honey was sitting back chilling at the table and smoking a joint. Ray rushed into the living room, scratching his head.

"I'm missin' some goddamn money," he said, looking around.

Almost immediately, Honey's eyes and mine connected. Ray then turned to Honey and cracked his knuckles.

"You got my money?" Ray asked. "I know you got it, so fess up!"

Honey moved his head from side to side. His eyes grew wide and he looked at me again. "I . . . I ain't got your money," he stuttered. "I swear I don't."

Ray moved closer to Honey. He stood right in front of him and looked down into his eyes. "Nigga, you wouldn't lie to me, would you? 'Cause see, fuckin' with my money is a serious crime around here. Son or no son, you may find yourself sniffin' dirt in the ground from stealin' from me. You get what I'm sayin', don't you?"

Surprisingly, Honey didn't appear as nervous as I thought he would be. I went into the kitchen and tried to throw Ray off. "You know Honey ain't been stealing no money from you, Ray. Back away from him and let's go. We gon' be late."

"There you go pokin' that big-ass nose of yours into matters that ain't got shit to do with you. I know damn well that I had forty dollars on my dresser in there and now it's gone."

I sighed from relief and so did Honey. This nigga was up in here acting a fool over forty dollars. Honey and me had already gotten him for several thousand. If he didn't notice that, too damn bad.

"You didn't put that forty dollars on the dresser," Honey said. "I saw it lying on the bathroom sink. Go look in there. I bet you'll find it."

Ray rushed off to the bathroom and came back with the forty bucks in his hand. He was all smiles. "I guess my mind been slippin', but that's what happens when you spend so many years with a dumb-ass bitch. Shit like that rubs off on a nigga, so make sure you get you one who smart as fuck." Ray looked at me. "Get yo' jacket and let's go."

Every single thing was my fault. I swear to God that he never, ever had anything nice to say about me. I grabbed my jacket and didn't bother to respond to Ray. Sometimes, ignorance needed to be ignored.

My gig had been paying off. Since I knew Honey had been taking money on the backend, I stepped it up, making all the money that I could make. Ray's dumb ass thought that I had been doing it all for him. He sat back at each gig, watching me with a big, bright smile on his face. I never paid him a bit of attention. I always flirted with the other niggas and shook my shapely ass well enough for them to dish out the paper. And trust me, they did. Lowdown, scum-ass niggas paid. Married niggas paid. Rich niggas paid and so did broke ones. They gave their last dimes, just to get a feel of what Ray considered his Money-Makin' Mama. He loved when the men turned to him, asking if I was his woman. With pride, he always answered yes.

"Yep, that's my bitch but you niggas already know the play. Touch, but keep yo' hard dicks in your pants or save them for the next ho."

While many of the men wished they could have sex with me, they wouldn't dare cross the line. I wasn't sure how much clout Ray had, nor did I understand why so many of these fools feared him. But money had power. Ray had power, and for now, whatever he said was a go.

On the drive home, Ray stared straight ahead and sucked his teeth. "I'm thinkin' about openin' a gentlemen's club. That way I may be able to serve up prime pussy, charge those niggas a substantial fee, and let them have at it. What do you think about that?"

"I can't believe you're asking for my opinion about anything. I'm sure that my opinion wouldn't even matter."

"If it didn't matter, I wouldn't have asked. And what's up with you lately? I've toned my shit down and you need to do the same damn thing too."

"Forgive me. I just have a lot on my mind right now. As for the club, look, do whatever you wish to do, Ray. All I ask is that you don't involve me. I'm getting kind of tired of doing this stuff, and since I only make a dollar a night, you know I'm not that damn enthused. I barely have money to buy maxi pads, and the last time I was in line to buy a bar of soap to wash my ass, I couldn't even afford it."

This time, Ray reached over and dropped a five dollar bill in my lap. "Consider that yo' raise. You need to stop bitchin' and gripin' all the time. While you may not have money in yo' hands, you still got a roof over yo' head. You got food, clothes, and water. You got a comfortable bed to sleep in at night and three nappy-head daughters to keep you busy. As for those maxi pads, I ain't seen you buy none of those in a while. Yo' ass ain't pregnant again, are you?"

I rolled my eyes and gazed out of the window. "Hell, no, I'm not."

"You'd better not be. 'Cause if you are, I know for sure it ain't mine. Just like those other kids you got. Don't none of them bitches look like me, not one. But this time around, if you're pregnant, that means you're pregnant by Miles. I promise you that I will beat that baby out of you and make you regret that you ever gave the pussy to him."

I turned to Ray and snapped, "Just so you know, I said I'm not pregnant. And Chyna, Karrine, and Simone are definitely your daughters. If you choose not to be their father, that's on you. Besides, you haven't been representing a decent damn daddy anyway."

Catching me off guard, Ray reached over and slapped the shit out of me. He had hit my nose, causing it to bleed. I caught the dripping blood with my hand and reached into my purse for some tissue.

"I told you to watch yo' mouth, didn't I?" Ray said. "When will you ever learn, TD? When will you ever fuckin' learn?"

For the next few minutes, my nose gushed blood. The moment we got home, I went into the bathroom to clean myself up. When I came out, Ray was sitting next to Chyna on the couch. He rubbed her hair and kissed her forehead.

"I changed my mind," he said. "She does look like me. Those other two, I'm not so sure."

Chyna looked straight ahead without saying a word. I hated to keep questioning her about Ray, and this time, when Ray went to the other apartment, I begged Chyna to tell me the truth.

"Please," I said to her. "If he's doing something—"

"Quit asking me that," she shouted. "Stop asking and leave me alone!"

Chyna rushed off to the bathroom and closed the door. It was obvious that I needed to hurry up and get the fuck out of there.

I was a nervous wreck. The plan was in motion, and I needed for Honey to come through for me in a major way. He asked three of his uncles to help him set this up. I didn't even know who the uncles were, nor was I sure if we could trust them.

"I got you," Honey said as we sat on the steps in the apartment complex, talking about tomorrow. "I promise you that everything gon' go down as planned and we gon' be set. Stop worrying, ma, all right?"

This kid not only had brains, but he also had a whole lot of guts. More guts than I'd had, because I couldn't stop thinking about what if something went wrong. What if Honey's uncle didn't follow through with the plan? What if they told Ray that it was all a set-up? I had a "trust no niggas" policy, so I didn't have as much faith as Honey did about all of this.

The next day, the girls were tucked in bed and put to sleep. I got dressed for my gig, and like always, I went to Ray's other apartment and waited for him. This time, I sat on the couch, waiting for Ray and Honey to get finished in the kitchen.

"Pass me that shit over there," Ray said to Honey. "I'ma need to spread a little love around tonight."

Honey passed Ray several of the tiny bags with little white rocks in them. They continued to work hard, until there was loud pounding on the door. Almost immediately, my heart dropped to my stomach. My palms started to sweat and there was a little shaking of my legs.

"Do you want me to get that?" I asked Ray.

"Naw, stay there."

Ray strutted to the door in his black suit and red tie that he intended to wear tonight. He looked through the peephole, and obviously not recognizing who the men were, he told Honey to toss him his gun that was on the table. Honey did so and that's when Ray approached the door again.

"Speak," he said.

"Lorenzo sent us to take care of that," one of the men said, using code to speak.

Hearing Lorenzo's name caused Ray to open the door. The second he did, the three men rushed in, knocking Ray down and yelling for me and Honey to hit the floor with our hands in the air so they could see them.

"Now, and don't none of you muthafuckas move!"

One of the men kicked Ray's gun away from his hand. He aimed his gun at Ray's temple and sent him a threat. "Place yo' hands behind your head, nigga! If you move, you die."

It was that plain and simple. Ray sat with his hands behind his head. I raised my hands in the air, and Honey rushed over to sit next to his father. He pretended to be scared and his body shivered all over. All I could say was the kid was one damn good actor.

"Please don't hurt us," Honey cried out. "Don't hurt my dad!"

One of the men pressed his gun against Honey's heaving chest. "Shut the fuck up, boy! Open yo' mouth again, and two holes gon' go into your daddy's head." He looked over at me. "Ho, get over here on the floor so I can keep my eyes on you."

I got so tired of being called a bitch that I kept my mouth shut and settled for being called a ho. I then rushed off the couch and joined Ray and Honey on the floor. I could tell that Ray's mind was racing, especially as he watched the men swipe the table clear of drug paraphernalia. They ransacked every room, cutting the sofa and mattresses and cleaning out every drawer. Ray was so sure that they wouldn't find out where his money was hidden, and when one of the men asked where it was, he refused to tell him.

"I don't have nothin' else. You niggas done took all that I got, so why don't y'all just get the fuck out here and call it a good day's work?"

"We'll leave when we have the money. Where in the fuck is it?" the man yelled through gritted teeth.

Ray shrugged, playing hard. Two of the men cocked their guns and aimed them directly at Honey's chest.

"By the time I count to three, if you don't tell us where the money is, we gon' blow several holes right through that li'l nigga's chest. My counting starts right now."

Ray sat with a smirk on his face. "Do what you got to do. I said I ain't got shit else, didn't I? Blowin' holes in his chest ain't gon' make no money appear."

I moved in front of Honey to shield and protect him. "No," I said as tears streamed down my face. "He's just a kid! He don't have nothing to do with this!"

"Do yo' ass know where the money is?"

Ray gazed at me, not knowing that I knew where the money was. Honey showed it to me several weeks ago. I slowly nodded and informed the man that I did know where it was.

"Then get off that big ass of yours and show me where it's at!"

I got up and Ray grabbed my wrist. "I know one thing. That is, you'd better not do what I think you're about to do. Sit the fuck down and shut yo' goddamn mouth."

I snatched my wrist away from Ray. "Beat my ass all you want to, Ray. This damn money ain't worth my life, yours, or Honey's. Shame on you for thinking that it is."

The man shoved my shoulder, telling me to move it. The other two stayed in the living room with Honey and Ray. I could hear Ray's loud mouth all the way in the other room. When one of the men told him to shut up, I also heard a loud thud. Since Ray didn't say anything after that, I suspected that he'd been hit in the mouth.

"Do your thing, baby," the man said to me as I stood in front of a bookshelf, filled with books. I removed several of the books then lifted a light switch that actually moved the bookshelf aside. Behind the bookshelf was a tiny room with metal shelves inside. On the shelves were stacks of money and several more guns. The young man smiled at me then yelled for another to come help.

"Go back in there and sit the fuck down," he said to me.

I did as I was ordered to do. Ray sat there with a mean mug on his face and a busted lip that was gushing blood. It was my pleasure to see him like this.

Within minutes, the men were in and out. Ray was on his feet, pacing the floor, yelling and screaming and acting a complete fool. The only person he could blame for this was me.

"As soon as I get back here tonight, I'ma beat yo' muthafuckin' ass for showin' them where my stash was! I can't believe this shit happened! How dare these niggas run up in here and take my shit from me!"

Ray was almost black as tar, but I swear his ass was turning red. Honey stayed silent and remained in a chair, as if he didn't know what the fuck was going on. I stood close by the door, trying my best to explain to Ray why I had revealed his stash. I already assumed that he'd be kicking my ass tonight, but I told myself that if everything went as planned, this would be the last time he'd ever put his hands on me again.

"What else was I supposed to do?" I fake cried and pounded my leg with my fist. "Do you not care about your only son? Did you want your daughters to be without a mother and a father? I just couldn't do that, Ray. I'm sorry, but I just couldn't do it!"

Ray walked up to me and punched me hard in my stomach. I doubled over and almost vomited from his blow being so hard. I coughed and held my aching stomach.

"Fuck you and those kids. I want my goddamn money back, and you best believe that somebody gon' have to answer for this shit. Maybe, that'll be you. Now, move out of my goddamn way so I can get the fuck out of here."

Ray stormed past me, grabbed his jacket, and left. From the inside, Honey and I could hear the screeching sound of Ray's tires as he sped off.

"Damn," Honey said in a soft, sad voice. "He was really gon' let them kill me. I'm glad they were really my uncles."

I hated to be the bearer of bad news, but Honey needed to know the truth about Ray. Bottom line, he wasn't shit.

"There is no loyalty whatsoever with him, Honey. I hope you know that by now. I don't know what that does to your relationship with him, but as long as you know who you're dealing with, you should be fine."

Honey smiled a little and wrapped his arms around my waist. I held him tight, knowing that he would be my right-hand li'l man for years and years to come.

Chapter Five

Later that night, and as expected, Ray came in drunk as hell and ready to fight. He beat my ass, but since I'd learned to fight his ass back, we made one big mess in the bedroom and caused a lot of ruckus. Gaping holes were in the wall, the window was broken, mirrors had been cracked, and shit was scattered everywhere. By morning, we sat across the kitchen table from each other, slowly chewing our food and staring without a blink. One of Ray's eyes was black and blue; so was mine. Bruises could be seen a mile away on both of us, but I was the only one with patches of my hair missing.

"You know what?" Ray said in a snobby tone. "I'm sick of yo' ass. Yo' pussy ain't about nothin' no more, and I ain't had no desire for it in a long, long time. I'm tired of payin' for somethin' that I don't really want, so why don't you get yo' ass up out of here and take those damn kids with you."

His words were like music to my ears. And while I was on my way up out of this mother-fucking apartment anyway, Ray made this easy for me. I pretended as if I still needed him. That way, he wouldn't suspect that I had anything to do with the robbery last night.

"Ray, stop this, okay? We . . . Where are me and the girls supposed to go? You know that I can't make it without you. I . . . I'll do my best to make things right, and I swear that I won't ever backtalk you again or fight back."

He slammed his hand on the table, shaking it. "Bitch, didn't you hear what the fuck I said? I ain't got time to listen to that bullshit story you tryin' to sell me. And as for those crocodile tears, you should've thought about that shit when you told them muthafuckas where my stash was at. And by the way, how in the hell did you know where it was anyway? I ain't ever told you, so how did you know? That nigga Honey told you, didn't he?"

I had to make this good, so I allowed a flood of tears to come out. I begged Ray not to release me from his life. "No, baby, no. Honey didn't tell me anything. He would never betray you like that. The only reason I knew was because I saw you go into the room a few times and move the shelf aside. For God's sake, Ray, rethink this and stop treating me like this. You gotta think about what would've happened if I didn't show them where the money was. We'd all be dead right now. I did what I thought was best, and to hell with that money."

Mentioning the money was a good way to get his blood boiling. He sucked in his bottom lip and bit into it. It was obvious that Ray loved his money more than anything else.

"I hate a beggin' bitch. And if you ever think I would choose my money over you, you got me fucked up." He shifted his eyes to the clock on the wall. "It's almost ten o'clock. You got until noon to get those few rags you got and get the fuck out of here."

I dropped to my knees and crawled over to him. "Please, Ray!" I begged. "Where am I gon' go? Don't do this to me, especially after all that I've done for you!"

I was damn good at pretending, and my performance was on point. Tears poured down my face, and I held on to Ray's leg as he got up from the table to walk away. He lifted his other foot and kicked my shoulder.

"Back the fuck up! You down there lookin' like a fuckin' stupid-ass dog. Get up and move it! Now, bitch, now!"

Okay, enough was enough. I sat on the floor, sobbing. Ray was clearly irritated by my actions and he couldn't take much more. He hurried to put on his clothes and got the hell out of there. Afterward, I got off the floor and smiled. I lit a cigarette and whistled smoke into the air, thinking about where I, my beautiful daughters, and handsome son would go from here.

Later that day, I waited at a nearby hotel with Honey. The girls were still at the apartment, so I had to hurry back to get them. Ray wanted us out, so therefore, I didn't have much time to waste.

We waited for Honey's uncles to arrive, and within the hour they came. They came in ready to negotiate with me, and I was so surprised when one of them asked for 70 percent of Ray's goods.

"Seventy percent?" I shouted while sitting on the couch with my legs crossed. "I don't think so. That's too damn much."

"Take it or leave it," one of the uncles said. "We did most of the work anyway."

"He's right," another said. It was apparent that they'd discussed this shit in the car. Their intentions were to get all that they could from the deal. "All y'all did was pretend to play scared and show us where to go."

Beforehand, none of us knew how much money was in Ray's secret room. Now that Honey's uncles were the only ones who knew, I suspected that they wouldn't be honest about the numbers, and fuck me. So in a sense, I was getting double fucked right now.

I stood and looked at the one who claimed that all we did was pretend and show him where the money was. "Pretend?" I said near tears. "Nigga, you were the one pretending, not me." I snatched off my shirt, causing the buttons to pop off and hit the floor. I displayed the numerous bruises on my chest, and pointed to a small stab mark that was visible on my side. "Does this shit look like I've been pretending? I've been getting my ass beat for almost ten fucking years! I have endured more goddamn pain and suffering than anybody you may ever know. What that nigga Ray did to me is worth every fucking penny that you all got out of that room and then some. So don't come up in here with no bullshit! Wrong bitch, wrong time!"

"I hear you, Miss Lady, but . . ."

I used my shirt to wipe the caked-on makeup from my face. Then I removed my jeans and stood in my panties, just so they could see the numerous bruises on my legs, where I'd been kicked over and over again. I had to be clear about this shit, and make them understand that I was having none of this shit.

"So, let's get back to this lack of work that I've done. I've been fucked in my ass and raped repeatedly, by a nigga who once told me he loved me. There have been times when my whole goddamn body has been covered with these bruises from head to toe, and if you look in my mouth, you will definitely find several missing teeth. My muthafucking daughters have been neglected and subjected to all of this bullshit, so please do not come up in here trying to fuck me, no more than I have already been fucked! Honey told y'all niggas that y'all were entitled to thirty percent of whatever was found. Seventy percent ain't happening, and neither is sixty, fifty, or forty. Thirty percent is what was offered and y'all are the ones who have to take that shit or leave it."

They all looked at each other and sat silent for a few minutes. One of the uncles finally spoke up. "I get what you're saying, and I'm sorry that you went through all that shit, but with it being three of us, we can't take no less than forty percent."

I got straight to the point and wasn't budging. "Thirty percent averages out to ten percent each.

Figure out a way to make it work." Niggas were always trying to get over. Not this time, hell no.

"Fine," one uncle said. "Thirty it is. I don't know how we're going to break all this dope down seventy/thirty, but I'm sure we'll figure out a way to do it. As for the money, there was roughly $1.6 million in that room. We'll make sure that you get yo' cut by tonight."

I looked at Honey who was shaking his head. "Naw, Uncle James, that ain't true," he said. "I used that machine and counted that money almost every single day. I know exactly how much was in there. It was $2,000,435. The change he had was shy fifteen cents of five thousand dollars. Y'all took the change too, didn't y'all?"

All I could do was smile. Honey had a bright-ass future ahead of him, and I'm sure he already knew it. All his uncles could do was sit there, look at each other, and contemplate a plan B.

"Let's settle this," I said. "If not, I'm gon' walk out that door right now and go tell Ray what actually happened to his money. All that's going to get me is another severe ass kicking. Something that I've gotten used to over time, so I'm pretty much numb to the shit right now. As for you niggas, well, I can't really say. But I will say that if the news about this hits the streets, it's not gon' look good for y'all. There are hating, backstabbing muthafuckas everywhere, and y'all will be forever watching y'all backs."

"Come on, Uncle Larry," Honey pleaded. "I thought we had a deal. If so, let's shake on it."

Honey held out his hand. And even though his uncles were reluctant to do it, they all shook his hand.

"Done deal," one said. "And yo' ass need to stop this hustling and get back in school. You ain't got no business getting involved in this kind of mess."

"What you talkin' about?" Honey said, bragging. "I do go to school. I'm an A plus student, and needless to say, I'm real good at math."

They all laughed and agreed to have the funds and dope to me later that evening. I plopped back on the couch, still in my panties. I swiped the sweat from my forehead, slowly but surely appreciating the no-nonsense bitch I was becoming.

Chapter Six

Needless to say, I was Ray McWilliams free! I mean, for whatever reason, he decided that he wanted to keep in touch with the girls from time to time. But whenever he visited with them, I was right there watching him. His relationship with Honey was just okay. Honey never forgot how Ray had chosen money over him, and it left a bad taste in his mouth. He was down with the person who remained loyal to him and that was me. Talk about being my nigga, Honey was it. I had mad love for him, but what we decided to do was keep our business endeavors a secret. No one ever found out that we were behind what had happened to Ray. He never recovered from losing that much money, nor did he know that his son and I had been secretly building an empire that was much bigger than the one he'd had. Day by day, we built that shit together. We worked hard, and Honey let these niggas out there know that he ran a no-nonsense business.

I was behind the scenes. Nobody knew what I'd been up to, not even my daughters who were now grown and much wiser than I was in my late twenties.

Thankfully, Karrine and Simone didn't remember a lot about what had happened in that apartment. They knew Ray as he was today. To me, he was still a conniving fool. I despised him with a passion, and when Chyna came forth one day and told me what he'd done to her, I could've died. I was so upset with her for not telling me that he used to come into the room the girls slept in, in the middle of the night, and have his way with her. He'd wait until I went to sleep then go do his dirt. The thing is, I always knew, deep in my heart, that he had been messing with my baby. And now that it was confirmed, there was no way possible for me to let that nigga live. The first person I broke the news to was Honey. I was staring out of the window with my arms folded.

"I know he's your father, but that nigga walking around here like he's such the perfect damn daddy and he ain't shit. I'm glad that Chyna finally told me what was up, and I honestly do not want him to take another breath on this earth."

Honey stood back on his bowlegs with his hands in his pockets. He then wiped down his sexy, chiseled face and stroked the hair on his chin. He was such a handsome young man, and at thirty years old, he had all of the chicks in the neighborhood throwing their pussies at him. He cocked his neck from side to side and cracked his knuckles.

"I'm not sure what to say," Honey said. "There are times when I still hang tight with the old man, but I don't like what he did to Chyna. That shit ain't cool at all."

"You're damn right it's not. And there ain't no way in hell for me to sit back and pretend that Chyna didn't confirm this. I've sat back long enough for years. Now, it's time for me to do something."

Honey stood for a while, thinking. He then walked to the door and touched the knob. "Look, do whatever you wish. Just know that this one won't be on me. I don't want to be included in the plans, nor do I want to know when or where the shit will take place."

"I wouldn't ask you to take care of this for me, but what I would like to know is if you're okay with me doing it? I don't want you to hold any grudges against me or be upset behind my actions. All I want you to do is understand why I have to do this. Chyna is my child, Honey, and I feel as though I failed her. This is how I must make this right. Please support me on this and allow me to make some kind of peace with it."

Honey released a deep sigh and stood for a few more minutes. He turned around then nodded. "Like I said, roll with it and do what you must. You have my full support. Don't you ever think that I don't understand what you and them girls went through. I witnessed some of it. Remember?"

I smiled because that's all the confirmation I needed. Honey walked out the door, and the following week, Ray was shot dead in his home. Shot in the face, five motherfucking times. No one knew who had done it. I figured that everyone would point their fingers at me, but I was at home cooking dinner for my lovely daughters. They could vouch for me, and I could vouch for them, especially Chyna who handled her business in a major way. I was very proud of her for ridding us of our number one enemy. And when I say that this shit felt good, I mean it. Ray's death felt good.

On the day of his funeral, I didn't shed one tear. I leaned over his casket, and while many people thought I had given him a kiss, what I did was gather a gob of spit in my mouth and spat it in his face. I then sat on a pew, thinking about all that nigga had done to me. He almost destroyed me, but the truth is, people don't change into who they are destined to be overnight. Experience is the best teacher, and whatever those experiences are, they mold and shape us "as is."

Now, I was proud to be Taffy Douglas. I didn't give two fucks about what people thought of me, not after what I'd been through, hell no. It might have taken awhile for me to break the grip that nigga had on me, but his grip was now gone. I couldn't be mad at the vital lessons our fucked-up relationship had taught me; after all, it enabled me to assist in preparing a smoother life for my girls. They'd have to go through some of the bull-shit out here too, but I endured years of pain with a no-good nigga so they wouldn't have to. I was able to share, in great detail, what that shit felt like. I broke down the rules for them, just so they wouldn't make the same mistakes. Somebody once said, "When you know better, you do better." And if you don't know, yo' ass better learn fast. I hipped my girls to the game. Showed them how to make money from grimy, horny, weak niggas who would give up their life savings, just to gaze at a piece of ass or watch a woman play with her pussy. The fools couldn't even touch them, but as long as the pussy looked good and asses clapped loudly, niggas were willing to pay.

There was no secret that I had developed disdain in my heart for fathers who didn't take care of their kids, for cowards who lied to women and disrespected them, and for fools who paid money to watch ass. At the end of the day, their money was good, and it helped us stay on top for quite some time. But being on top in the drug game, and being without Ray, wasn't the end of my story. Actually, it was just the beginning . . .

Part Two

The Beginning

Chapter Seven

Taffy

"Don't know no love, don't show no love," was what I taught my three girls Chyna, Karrine, and Simone. The only love we had was for each other. Our bond as mother and daughters was unbreakable.

I'd been schooling my girls on this thing called life since the day I screamed out like a madwoman and forced them out of my coochie. I didn't want my baby girls to hook up with any nigga who was like their deadbeat-ass daddy. I wanted them to hook up with a motherfucker who would respect them. One who they could love because he had their backs and they could count on him to provide for them every step of the way. One who could have them riding around in a Mercedes, Range Rover, or Bentley, as they all did right now. One who could take them on trips from the Bahamas to Africa, if they chose to go there. I mean, this dude had to come correct. But the only nigga who could be down with my daughters in a way that I expected him to be, he went by the name of money.

Yes, that's right. I taught my daughters to fall in love with money. Money was the only thing that could give them what no other mother-fucker could. It provided for them like no other and swept them off their goddamn feet. They were high off money, instead of being fucked up in the head because some damn fool done broke their hearts, done them wrong, or cheated on them. It was my job as Mama to make sure my girls didn't go down the same path as I had traveled. Getting their asses beat just because and getting kicked out of the crib because a man told you you had to go, that wasn't where it was at. I had my stories to tell and you'd better believe that I told my daughters exactly what kind of father they'd had. They were now well aware, but Karrine and Simone had a little soft spot for him in their hearts. Not Chyna, though. She hated that motherfucker. She had every right to.

When Chyna turned twenty-six, she did her Mama a big favor. I'll never forget it, and I owed her big time for handling something that I could or should have taken care of years ago.

That day, Chyna had gone to the beauty shop early in the morning to get her hair braided. Like me, she wore long braids that flowed down her back and almost touched her apple bottom big booty that was the most money producing ass in the house. While my braids sat wrapped tightly on my head, Chyna's were parted through the middle. She had a round face that displayed her rich chocolate skin. Her body was sculptured like a goddess, and all of my girls' curvy hips were enough to turn any man's or woman's head. There was no secret that Chyna and I were the closest out of me and my girls, because Chyna did shit for me that the other two might not do. She had my back. Anything that I asked her for she would do it.

She left the beauty shop around six o'clock that evening and called me on her way to Ray's place. He had no idea she was coming and he had told the girls that if they ever stopped by they needed to call before they came. The only reason he required that was because he didn't want any of them to confront his bitches. The last time Simone was at his house, she beat the mess out of his side ho, Tracy, who didn't know when to keep her mouth shut. He didn't want the girls to catch him in the act of running his drug store. My girls were no fools, and it didn't take a rocket scientist to figure out what Ray was doing. I'll just say that a motherfucker who dropped out of school in the eighth grade didn't have many options. Ray was a fifty-five-year-old man, but he liked bitches who were much younger than he was.

At forty-six my pussy was all dried up, according to him, so he didn't want no part of me anymore. He considered me washed up way before then, but that was his opinion, not mine. I was happy about that because he could lay those ass kickings on somebody else. All the cheating was left for another bitch to deal with, and he had done me a favor when he kicked me out on my ass and told me to never come back.

The only thing that I didn't like was when he disrespected my daughters. When Simone fought his trick, Tracy, Ray took her side and put his hands on my baby. That didn't work for me either, and I really had to put a plan in action to get rid of his ass, especially after he molested Chyna.

After that day, I knew what I had to do. It was inevitable and timing was everything. I plotted revenge with Chyna and only her. Simone and Karrine were wussies when it came to Ray. They let him get away with too much shit, as I had done. I didn't like that one bit, because what you allow yo' daddy to do, you will allow any man to do. So without nobody knowing it, Chyna handled things like only she knew how.

She called me on the phone while I was cooking fish for dinner in the oversized kitchen in our townhouse. It was spacious, with four bedrooms and three levels. I slept in the upstairs bedroom, Chyna slept on the lower level, and Simone and Karrine shared the second floor. We all had privacy. That was a good thing because I didn't want my girls to think I was crowding their space. As I turned the crispy fish cooking in hot grease, Chyna whispered to me.

"Mama, are you still there?"

"Yes, I am, Chyna. I was just trying to finish dinner."

"Well, I just parked in front of his house. I want you to hear this shit go down, so don't hang up."

I didn't hang up, but I put the phone on speakerphone so I could get done cooking before Simone and Karrine came home. I wanted Chyna to have something to fill her belly with too. Lord knows she deserved it. We had planned this for months. Chyna wanted to do this, and out of all of my kids, she was the brave one. I couldn't think of a better person to kill that fool, and as we discussed it, Chyna seemed hyped. If or when the cops asked questions, I would be her alibi, and she would be mine. And if that wasn't good enough, we already had a friend of mine, Phatty, who agreed to say she was right here with us having dinner. I suspected that the police wouldn't dig too deep. As much trouble as Ray had been in, I figured that they wanted his ass off the streets just as much as we did.

"I'm makin' my way to his door now," Chyna said. "You wanna hear me knock?" she joked.

"Girl, would you stop playing? This is some serious shit and yo' ass needs to be careful. Ray got all kinds of guns and shit up in there. I don't want you to get hurt."

"He trusts me, Mama, so I'll be fine. And if all else fails, all I have to do is fuck him and he'll get with the program."

Chyna touched a nerve. I halted what I was doing and stood still. That was another thing about Ray. He had hurt Chyna when she was seven years old, but Chyna never told me that he had come into her bedroom to have sex with her until years later. I stood stone-faced, thinking about the day she told me what Ray had done to her.

Chyna had just gotten home from high school. I was chilling back on the couch, watching TV while talking to one of my girlfriends about a fucked-up date she'd been on. But when I saw the horrified look in Chyna's eyes, I told Nicole I'd have to call her back and hung up the phone.

"Chyna," I yelled out to her as she headed toward her room. "Come back here. What's wrong with you?"

"Nothing!" she hollered from the other room.

I smashed my cigarette in an ashtray then got off the couch to go see what was up. I suspected that she was having issues with some of those bad-ass, knucklehead boys from school, but I wasn't sure. I didn't understand why they always picked on my damn kids, and I got tired of going to their school threatening those muthafuckas. Obviously, my threats weren't working.

As Chyna sat on the bed with her head hanging low, I stood in the doorway with my arms crossed. "What happened at school today?"

"Nothing," she said without looking up at me.

"Something had to happen because you wouldn't be sitting there looking like a sad puppy. If those boys are still fucking with you, just tell me. I warned them before, and if I have to blow another hole in their asses for fucking with you I will."

"They ain't messing with me no more. I told you it was nothing."

I walked farther into the room then sat on the bed next to Chyna. That's when I noticed a small bruise underneath her eye. My heart sank to my stomach. I reached for her chin, and quickly turned her face toward me.

"What happened to your face?" My tone had gone up a notch. Chyna knew better than to lie to me.

"I tripped and fell—"

"Tripped and fell my ass, Chyna!" I let go of her face then jumped to my feet. I then reached for her hand, attempting to pull her off the bed. "Let's go. Take me to whoever did that to you. I don't care how young his ass is. If he's brave enough to hit you then I'ma be bold enough to put my foot in his ass."

I yanked Chyna's arm but she resisted. "Let me go, Mama. I don't want to go anywhere. Just leave me alone and stop trying to embarrass me!"

My mouth dropped open. "Embarrass you? I don't give a damn if you're embarrassed by me. If you don't know how to stand up for your fucking self, then I'm going to stand up for you. All of this needs to stop, Chyna. I've been to the school, talked to those boys' parents, and I'm sick of being nice. You can't expect me to sit back and do nothing."

Chyna still didn't budge, so I left her ass sitting there near tears. I knew where to go to get the answers I needed, and one of Chyna's friends down the street was the one who told me about those boys messing with my girls last time. Surely she knew something, so I was on my way to see her. But as I made my way to the door, Chyna called out to me. Displaying rage, I swung around, mad at her for not speaking up, but very sympathetic to my child who I knew was hurting from the tears she started to shed.

"I . . . It's not those boys who keep messing with me," Chyna said with her head hanging low again. She kept fidgeting and didn't dare to look me in the eyes.

"Who in the hell is it then? Tell me who put their goddamn hands on you."

There was a sharp, long silence before Chyna softly whispered, "Ray."

I frowned, thinking that I misunderstood her. "Ray who?"

"My daddy. He chased after me because I refused to get in the car with him. I didn't want to go with him. Not this time. I just couldn't do it."

"Go with him where? And what made him hit you?"

Chyna shrugged. "I guess the same thing that always made him hit you."

Her words stung. I walked back over to the bed and sat next to Chyna again. She wasn't telling me the whole story, and deep down, I feared there was so much more to this. I pushed and pushed for Chyna to tell me more. That's when more tears started to fall, and she said something to me that damn near took every single breath out of me.

"He touched me, Mama. Been touching and feeling on me, ever since I was seven years old. I'm tired of him doing nasty things to me, and a father ain't supposed to do that kind of stuff to his own daughter, is he?"

I sat as if cement had been poured over me. My lips felt locked together. Goosebumps were all over my arms, and there was a pain in my stomach that felt as if Mike Tyson had punched me in it. I slowly turned my head to look directly into Chyna's eyes. I already knew she wasn't lying to me, and the thought never crossed my mind. For years, I had suspected that Ray had done something to her. But every time I asked, she denied it. She brushed it off, and just a few months ago she told me I was out of my mind for thinking such a thing. I didn't bother to ask what made her speak up now. It didn't matter.

What mattered was I knew. I'd heard every word my daughter had just told me, and she didn't have to go into further details about it. At that point, I knew that Ray had to die.

I held Chyna in my arms, allowing her to cry hard on my shoulder. I cried too, but not in front of her. It was later that night when I sat on the edge of my bed with a Glock 9 shaking in my hand. Ray was supposed to come over, and I waited for him to come through the door so I could blow his fucking brains out. I didn't need the police, and I didn't want to tell anyone what had happened. Putting him behind bars wasn't good enough for me. He needed to be six feet under; there was no other option. With that in mind, I waited. Waited for hours, but Ray was a no-show. I called his phone; he didn't answer. Called around looking for him; nobody knew where he was. And by four o'clock in the morning, I finally realized that maybe it was a good thing that he didn't come. My daughters would've witnessed a murder that they definitely didn't need to see. They would see me in handcuffs, and knowing that they'd be thrown in the foster care system woke me up. This was something I had to plan for. I had to be real careful, and then execute a plan that would wash that nigga off this earth. I finally smiled that night while thinking about how I wanted it done.

I had never forgiven myself for what had happened to Chyna, but today that nigga was going to pay for all the hurt he'd inflicted on me and my girls. Maybe some people thought I was a coward for not smoking his ass myself, but that was in no way the case.

If Ray was killed, 99 percent of the people would think I'd done it. No one would ever suspect Chyna, but if they did suspect either of us, we both were covered. I, myself, was at home, cooking some seasoned catfish and coleslaw for me and my girls. If I needed an alibi, I had some.

I heard Chyna knock on Ray's door.

"Who is it?" Ray shouted.

"It's me, Ray. Chyna."

Less than ten seconds later, I heard a firecracker sound pop five times through my speakerphone. I tightened my stomach to cool the queasy feeling I had, but when I heard Chyna's voice, I could tell everything had gone as planned.

"Done," was all she said.

"Good. Now come home. Mama got something real good waiting for you."

"I don't want fish," she said. "I want chicken."

Yeah, sometimes my daughters were some ungrateful bitches, but I loved them nonetheless. "Chicken it is then," I said. "Anything you want."

Right then and there, Chyna had earned her badge of honor from me. We never told Simone or Karrine shit, and when they heard about Ray being killed, they took the news real hard. Even at his funeral they could barely look at him and they couldn't stop crying. With my black silk dress on that squeezed my size forty double-Ds and cut above my knees, I had no problem looking at him. While nobody was looking, I leaned down into his casket and pretended to give him a sweet kiss on the cheek. Instead, I spat in that motherfucker's face and said good riddance to the nigga I hated the most on this earth.

Chapter Eight

Karrine

"Mama!" I yelled from the bottom stair while looking up at her bedroom. She said she was going to take a shower, but I needed some answers right here and now.

I had been in downtown Chicago at a new nightclub that had just opened last night, and I saw Ray's down chick, Tracy, who Simone had beef with. She and a gang of bitches she was with started looking my way, but since Simone or Chyna didn't go with me, I was pretty much on my own. My girl, Lylah, was with me, but she wasn't the type of bitch to have my back. Only my sisters were, so I knew when it was smart for me to clamp my mouth shut and make a move before some shit went down. On my way out, one of the chicks whispered some noise in my ear about Chyna killing Ray. And when I asked Chyna what was up a few minutes ago, she jerked her head in another direction and refused to answer me.

Something was up. I could feel it. The rule was for us to never lie to each other and all I wanted to know was the truth. Shit like that didn't just hit the streets out of nowhere. Somebody knew something and the best person to shut this noise down was Mama.

She didn't answer me when I yelled up the winding staircase that led to her bedroom, but I could hear the shower running. I went back into my room where Simone was typing something on the computer, and Chyna's big booty self was lying across my bed still ignoring me. There was no question that I loved my older sister to death, but I could never take her lying to me. We weren't supposed to get down like that, so I asked her again what the fuck the chick with Tracy was talking about.

Chyna tossed her braids to the side and sat against the headboard on my queen-sized bed that was accessorized with a metallic gold ensemble. I had a thing for gold and 70 percent of all my clothes and shoes had a hint of gold in them. Even my Mercedes that I referred to as the love of my life was gold. It was like that for me, and Mama hated it because she thought the color gold did me no justice. I was lighter than my other two sisters. They were a delightful chocolate brown. My hair was nearly shaved off, but what little I did have had a blond tint. My thin, almond-shaped eyes lured in many niggas, and the look in my seductive eyes benefited me in my profession. I could make a nigga bust a nut just from him staring into my eyes. My brows looked painted on and were perfectly arched. I was the only sister who went with the natural look and weave didn't do shit for me. As for makeup? Not a drop of it was needed, but I sometimes used foundation to cover up a black mole on my cheek that was sexy, but too noticeable.

"I wish you would stop askin' me questions about Ray," Chyna said, flipping through a magazine. "Whoever fucked him up is probably long gone. All I can say is it wasn't me."

"Come over here and look at this," Simone whispered and interrupted us talking. She was still on the Internet and had been for the last hour.

We rushed over to see what was up. What we saw was a $2,000 deposit that had gone into Simone's bank account. For somebody to pay her that kind of money, they wanted something heavy to go down. We all made a decent living doing video porn and paper had been falling down on us like rain.

I had my own Web site and Chyna and Simone had theirs. Then we had a combined Web site where all three of us provided a service all at once. It was no secret that Chyna made the most money, then I did. Simone had some catching up to do, and there were times when we competed against each other to see who could make the most paper. Most of the time Chyna won. Simone had won one or two times, but I was never far behind. My body was sculptured like a Coca-Cola bottle and my ass wasn't no jumbo booty, but it was perfect. Simone wasn't as blessed as me and Chyna was, but Mama didn't raise no chicks who couldn't use what they had to make the kind of money we'd been bringing in.

The good thing about Internet porn was we didn't have to get physical with nobody and we avoided getting any sexually transmitted diseases. All we had to do was put on a show and bring pleasure to the men who watched us from the other side and, sometimes, gave us orders to do things that pleased them.

These men consisted of drug dealers, married men, politicians, athletes: you name it. Our clientele was thick. Most of the escapades took place after nine o'clock at night and there were times when we'd be up until three or four in the morning showing off what Mama had blessed us with.

"Two thousand dollars," I said, reading limited instructions the man who went by the name of Honey had left Simone. He wanted her all to himself at ten o'clock sharp tonight.

I playfully pushed her shoulder. "Girl, you'd better work hard for that money, especially if he payin' like that. Ain't no tellin' how much his next offer may be."

"Right," Chyna said. "And if you need any tips, be sure to let me know. I'll show you how to work it, no doubt."

Chyna popped her booty and we all laughed. I swear I loved my sisters. The profession we were in didn't bother us one bit, and there wasn't too many people who could actually say they loved their job. Even though I wasn't a virgin, Simone claimed that she still was. She said that she was saving herself for the right nigga to come along, but she didn't know her business was already in the streets. She'd fucked a baller named Reno, and he told everybody that he'd busted Simone's cherry. She didn't know that we knew what was up, and for sisters who weren't supposed to lie and keep secrets from each other, I guessed there were some things we were willing to keep to ourselves.

If Mama had any say-so about men, none of us would have any relationships at all. Whenever we did hook up with somebody we had to do that shit on the side. No serious dating was allowed, but that was no problem for me because I hadn't met anybody who tickled my fancy enough and made me want to fall in love with them. Neither had Chyna. Then again, she was known for doing sneaky shit that nobody ever knew about. If you asked she'd tell you, but what you didn't ask you were left to assume.

"I gotta find me somethin' real sexy to wear," Simone said, pulling her weaved-in long and wavy hair over to one shoulder. She smiled while looking at the computer monitor and seemed excited about the $2,000 payout that would only cost her thirty minutes of her time.

"What y'all doing in there?" Mama asked as she came into the room with her housecoat on. She had a slight cold because the weather in Chicago kept changing by the day. One day it was snowing, the next day it was hot enough to go swimming and walk your dog in the park.

Simone pointed to the computer monitor, showing Mama her recent deposit. Mama's eyes grew big. "Damn! Who did that?"

"His name is Honey. This my first time seein' his deposit, but I'll get a chance to check him out tonight."

Yep, Mama knew how we got down. Who in the hell do you think hipped us to this shit? She used to do it, and it was nothing for Mama to make anywhere from $5,000 to $10,000 a week, shaking her ass in front of the computer and teasing men. She still did a little something every now and then, but since we were banking together about $10,000 a week, Mama could lay low and depend on us to hold things down for her. She never asked for one penny of our money. What little we did give to her, it helped pay the bills.

"Make sure I see him before you do your thing," Mama said. "I want to make sure it ain't the same nigga Honey I had some dealings with before."

"Honey who?" I asked. "Why you always talking in circles? And what kind of dealings are you talking about?"

"I meant Harry, not Honey, so forget what I said. And if anybody be talking in circles, that would be you, not me."

Mama ignored me then looked at Simone. She got up from the chair, rushing into her walk-in closet to see what she could put on that was overly sexy.

"Did you hear me callin' you earlier, Miss Lady?" I said to Mama.

She sat on my bed and lit a cigarette. While holding it with her perfectly manicured nails, she took a puff from the Virginia Slim then whistled smoke into the air. "I ain't heard nothing. What did you want?"

I crossed my arms, displaying a little attitude. "I got a question for you. Do you know anything about Ray's murder? Word on the street is Chyna had somethin' to do with it. I hope that ain't true."

Mama's eyes shifted to Chyna then she blinked and looked down at her nails.

I stomped my foot and pouted. "Come on, Mama, tell me the truth. I need to know what's up. I hope to God it ain't true."

"And what if it was?" Chyna said. Her voice was laced with much attitude and seriousness was washed across her face. "What difference does it make? He wasn't shit no way, and what did he ever do for us? I can't believe you and Simone shed all those tears at that man's funeral. Whoever knocked his ass off, good for them."

Mama held a smirk on her face, as if Ray's death pleased her to the fullest. Simone saw it too, and she eased out of the closet to listen in. She pretended to be on the shy side, but I knew better. Money made her loosen up, and she got the biggest thrill out of how we made a living.

"Don't be talkin' about Ray like that," I said to Chyna. "At the end of the day he was our daddy. He may not have been the best father in the world but—"

Mama's smirk vanished. She quickly cut me off and raised her voice. "Karrine, stop talking about that man like he was some goddamn saint. That nigga didn't do nothing for y'all, and I'm with Chyna on this. Whoever shot his ass, good for them. They did all of us a favor. Now, I don't want to hear shit else about it."

I was getting angry. Talking about Ray like that was a touchy subject because he, at least, gave us money when we didn't have nothing. Mama didn't always do her thing on the Internet, and when we were little, I remember how rough shit was. Ray was the one who brought paper into the house and put food on the table. He kept a roof over our heads, even though the tiny apartment we lived in was fucked up.

"Okay, fine," I said, walking over to my bed and sitting on it. "Now that both of y'all got that off y'all's chests, can somebody be honest with me about what really happened to Ray? I can tell by the look in y'all eyes that something ain't right around here when his name comes up."

While giving me a hard stare, Mama tightened her lips around the tip of the cigarette to suck in more smoke. She blew the smoke into my face, and then got up and left the room. Chyna rolled her eyes at me and followed Mama. All Simone did was shrug her shoulders, and then she went back into the closet to search for something to put on.

Chyna and Mama had gone to the kitchen, so I went in there, only to see them whispering to each other. I interrupted their conversation.

I folded my arms, still edging them on about what had happened to Ray. "We don't keep secrets, do we? We don't lie to each other, do we? We protect each other and have each other's backs, don't we? I thought that's how it was. And what about you sayin' there will be no surprises?"

"Karrine, please don't do this," Mama said, standing by the kitchen counter. "For the last time, just let it go."

I pounded my fist against my leg. "I don't want to let it go. I need to know the truth and somebody needs to tell me what that is right now."

I pouted more, even though I could see the devilish gaze in Mama's eyes that I didn't like to see. *Man, just tell me what the fuck is going on and be done with it. Is it that hard to do?* The answer was either yes or no.

As Mama started to fire back at me, Simone came into the kitchen with a black teddy thrown across her arm.

"Do you really and truly want to know the truth?" Mama hollered out. "I don't think you're ready for it, especially since you think your fucking daddy was all that!"

"I'm not sayin' he was all that!" I bravely yelled back. "What I'm sayin' is he didn't deserve to be shot by no coldblooded killer! I want to know if my sister is that damn coldblooded, where she can shoot her own father in the chest five motherfuckin' times!"

Mama yanked on the kitchen drawer to open it, and then snatched a knife from inside of it. She charged up to me then placed the sharp blade against the side of my neck. From the corner of my eye, I could see Simone shaking and standing in fear. She didn't dare move another inch and neither did I. Sweat started to dot my forehead and anger crept up on me so fast that I almost couldn't hold back. Chyna moved closer and reached out to try to remove the knife from Mama's hand.

"Back the fuck up," Mama yelled at Chyna. "If this heifer wants the truth, I'ma give it to her. But before I do . . ." She pressed the blade harder against my neck. More sweat had started to form on my forehead and it dripped along the sides of my face. I didn't dare move. Barely wanted to breathe. If I did move, there was a chance the blade would slice me.

Mama spoke through gritted teeth. "Don't you ever raise your voice at me again. You got that, bitch?"

I slowly nodded. The one thing none of us did was play around with Mama. I must've been tripping when I raised my voice. She didn't deal with disrespect. There were very few times that I'd tried her, but I wound up getting my feelings hurt. For now, all I wanted to find out was the truth about Ray. Finally, she spilled it.

"The truth and nothing but the truth is Ray wasn't shit and he deserved to die. You weren't there, Karrine, when he put his dick in my child's mouth and make her swallow his goddamn semen. You weren't there when he stole her innocence, fucked her in the ass, and made her bleed, so how dare you stand there and defend that son of a bitch! For years, I wanted to kill that motherfucker myself, but I couldn't do it. And if my baby girl found the guts to wipe that nigga off the face of the earth, so be it. What you need to know is we will not be having this conversation again. Chyna doesn't owe anybody an explanation about what she did and why! Do you got that, heifer? 'Cause if you don't, it's gon' be me and you. I doubt that you want that to happen."

By now, tears were welled in my eyes and my breathing was heavy. Chyna rarely ever cried, but the mean mug on her face showed just how upset she was. Simone walked slowly over to Mama and held out her hand.

"Put the knife down, Mama," she said softly. "All Karrine did was ask a question. Now that we have our answer, let's all just let it go."

"It's done," I said too. "And thank you for bein' honest with me."

The cold look in Mama's eyes had chilled, just a little. She laid the knife on the counter and shot me a dirty glimpse before she walked away. The last thing I wanted was to have a beef with her. Something about that didn't seem right to me. I felt as though I owed her a sincere apology.

"You ain't gotta get all mad about it," I shouted out to her, trying to joke around. Mama had a heart. She loved us to death. It hurt her more to do what she had just done to me; I already knew it.

She turned around before going upstairs. "I did have to get mad about it, Karrine. Don't try me like that again. Never again or I will slice your fucking throat."

I didn't doubt it, and I would do my best not to go there with her again. But with the way all of us were, there wasn't no telling when we would find ourselves in another one of these situations again.

Chapter Nine

Simone

I was glad that Mama and Karrine squashed their beef with each other. The most important thing right now was to make sure Chyna was all good, and to see what was up with this nigga Honey. My sisters and Mama thought I was the shy one, but they were so wrong about me. I knew when to keep it cool. I also knew when it was time to show my ass. That time wasn't when Mama had a knife near Karrine's throat. I wasn't sure if she was going to use it. She had never done anything to that magnitude before, but we all knew that Mama could be a motherfucker if you rubbed her the wrong way.

I didn't understand why Karrine kept pushing her, but I bet she wouldn't do that shit again. I wanted to know the truth about Ray too, but after hearing what he had done to Chyna, I was mad as hell. Had I known what he'd done to her, I would have shot that nigga myself, cut his dick off, and shoved it into his mouth. I know Mama had told us not to talk about it, but as soon as we got back to Karrine's room, we talked about it. Mama was in her bedroom, but we whispered to each other so she wouldn't hear us discussing it and trip.

"I didn't know Ray did all that shit to you," I said to Chyna as she sat on Karrine's bed.

"It was a long time ago. I'm over it. I feel much better now that his ass is six feet under, sniffin' dirt."

The only reason I laughed was because she did. Chyna was strong and she held all of us down. She had all of our backs, and I couldn't help but to think about a time when she almost got killed because of me.

It started with what was supposed to be a quick visit to the grocery store. Mama said she needed some butter and eggs to make a cake and I told her I would go to the store and get it. Chyna decided to ride along with me, and on the way there, we chatted in the car about feelings she was catching for this ugly dude at school. Body wise, he was hooked up. But his face wasn't about nothing.

"That nigga look like he been beat in the face with several bats. I know you can do better than him. You just like him because he's a star football player, that's why."

"That may have a little something to do with it, but he still cute. Look way better than that Nico dude you be following around, and if anybody ugly, it's that trick he be with all the time. Are they a couple or what?"

"I'm not sure, but I don't be following anybody around. His ass be sniffing after me; you can trust and believe that."

We laughed, and as soon as we got to the grocery store, we just happened to see Chance, the ugly dude Chyna had a crush on.

"See?" I said to Chyna as we walked down the aisle laughing. "You talked up on him, didn't you? Why don't you go say something to him?"

Her face twisted. "Say something like what? It ain't that serious and you know I'm not about to confront no dude about my feelings."

"You don't have to confront him. All you have to do is go walk in front of him and let your big ass speak for you. Your face can speak for you, too, and I know you ain't trying to be shy up in here."

"Now is not the time or the place. Why don't you go get the butter and I'll go get the eggs?

That way we can hurry up and get the hell out of here."

I walked off to get the butter, but as soon as I grabbed a stick of butter, I saw Chance again. This time, he was standing next to two other dudes who were looking my way. I always like attention, so I took it upon myself to go find out what all the stares were about. I also wanted to put a few words in Chance's ear about Chyna liking him.

"Sup," I said, approaching Chance and his friends. "Why y'all staring so hard?"

One of the niggas was real blunt. "Bitch, ain't nobody staring at you. I was checking out that fine-ass white gal behind you."

I turned around, seeing no one in sight. "I don't see anyone there, but obviously there was someone nearby because she must've been the bitch instead of me."

Trying to keep the peace, I walked away. But after only a few steps, the same nigga had the audacity to come up from behind me and grab at my breast. Before I knew it, I lifted my hand and smacked the living daylights out of him. He didn't hesitate to respond to my slap, and in a matter of seconds, he pushed me so hard that I fell backward and knocked down a display of cupcakes. Many people looked to see what was going on, especially when Chance's friend started using more profanity.

"That's what you get, bitch! And every time I see you, from here on out, I'ma fuck you up, just for putting your hands on me."

I could barely get off the floor, before I saw Chyna rush up from behind with the eggs in her hand. She smashed them clean in the nigga's face then kicked his ass right in the nuts. He grabbed his dick and quickly dropped to his knees.

"Fuuuuuck," he shouted. "What the fuuuuuck!"

Chance and his other friend looked at Chyna who dared them to say or do anything to her. They ignored her and helped their friend off the floor. By that time, security was there and all of us were asked to leave the store. I was pissed and embarrassed at the same time. Everybody looked at us as if we'd stolen something. I even tried to tell the security guard what had happened, but he didn't want to hear it.

"Just get out of here and don't come back. You people are always somewhere causing trouble."

"You people?" Chyna responded before I did. "What in the hell do you mean by that?"

He didn't respond, but for the next ten minutes or so, Chyna stood there going off on him and cursing his ass out.

"You have two minutes to leave this store, young lady, or I'm calling the police. Go now and never, ever come back!"

The man pointed to the door. I definitely didn't want to go to jail, so I tugged at Chyna's arm, dragging her out the store so we could leave. She continued to put up a fuss, but within a few minutes, we walked outside together. As soon as we stepped on the parking lot, we heard screeching tires and saw a burgundy car coming our way. I had already moved out of the way, but Chyna was too busy squinting, trying to see who was behind the wheel. By the time she realized who it was, it was almost too late. Chance's friend was behind the wheel, and he was only a few feet away from hitting Chyna. She dove on top of somebody's car to avoid herself from being hit. I ducked behind the car, and as those niggas sped off the parking lot, we could hear them laughing.

"Stupid bitches!" Chance yelled out the window. "We should've killed yo' ass!"

The car sped away, and it took everything I had in me not to jump in my car and follow them.

"Let them niggas go, Simone," Chyna said. "They'll get what's coming to them, just not today. I need to get home and wash this off."

I looked down at Chyna's knee, which was dripping blood. When she dove on the car, she scraped her knee real bad and an open gash was visible. I wasn't sure if I should take her home or to the hospital. And when I asked, she said home.

"Are you sure? That looks like you may need some stiches."

"Fuck stitches. Take me home so I can clean this up. I'll be okay."

"Okay, but I still think I need to take you to the doctor. When we get home, let Mama see it so she can tell you what she thinks."

"I don't care what she thinks. I don't need a damn doctor, so will you hurry up and go get the car? I don't think I can walk on it right now."

"Is it broken?"

"Stop asking questions and go get the car. Please."

I rushed to go get the car then helped Chyna get inside. On the drive home we didn't say much to each other. Chyna looked pissed, though, and I felt as if all of this was my fault. If I had never stopped to confront those dudes, none of this would've happened. I should have got my damn butter and went on about my business.

The second we got home and told Mama what had happened, she wound up taking Chyna to

*the hospital. My big sis had a broken leg and
didn't even cry about it. She wasn't even mad at
me either, and Lord knows I felt terrible. I told
her how sorry I was, but all she did was laugh it
off while sitting on the hospital bed.*

*"Girl, whatever. Shit happens, and you can
be sure that the crush I had on Chance no longer
exists."*

*"I hope not, 'cause as I said before, that is one
ugly dude. You can definitely do better than
that."*

*Chyna held out her hand, slapping it against
mine. "You're damn right I can. And shame on
me for thinking that he was all that."*

*We laughed, but when Mama entered the
room, we quickly got silent. We'd told her that
some crazy niggas tried to run Chyna over, but
we definitely didn't tell her how the incident
really started. I laughed to myself, thinking
that some things never changed. Lies to Mama
were ongoing, and Chyna, like always, forever
had my back.*

And after reflecting on the past, I couldn't
even imagine what Ray had done to her. Chyna,
however, cut me off as I started to talk about it
again. She looked at Karrine then back to me.

"I'll repeat what Mama said. We done talkin'
about this, and please don't tell nobody that that

shit happened to me. When y'all bring it up, I have to relive it. That's not what I want to do. So for me, change the subject."

"Please do," Mama said, coming into the room. Like normal she was dressed in black. She rocked a black pantsuit with no shirt underneath. Her cleavage was showing and her high heels gave her plenty of height. She never removed the braids from being wrapped into a bun on her head and she dazzled up her pretty face with rose-colored makeup. Mama was a beautiful woman and it was because of her that we all carried good looks. She was thick, though, but her thickness was in all the right places.

"I need to check out of here and go have a drink. Maybe I'll be back later; maybe I won't. Either way don't wait up for me. I'll have my cell phone if y'all need me."

Whenever Mama had something on her mind, she fled. It's what she did just so she didn't have to get in our shit about something. Karrine had seriously fucked up, but when she yelled out to Mama that she loved her, Mama said it back.

"You know love, but don't show love, unless it's for me and your sisters. Have fun tonight and don't y'all hurt nobody."

Mama left Karrine's room. And for now, things seemed to be back to normal. Karrine and Chyna didn't have Internet "dates" until after ten, but I had to get prepared for my escapade with Honey.

"Bye, y'all," I said, waving as I left Karrine's bedroom and went to mine. My room was across the hallway from hers. She chose to lay her room out with gold, but like Mama, I was more of a red, white, and black chick. Black silk sheets covered my bed and red cottony pillows were strewn on top of my bed. Black and red beads created a backdrop behind my bed because I preferred not to utilize a headboard. Fuzzy red, white, and black rugs covered my floors, but the most exciting thing about my room was my computer desk that held up a thirty-inch monitor I used to show these niggas what was up.

With the monitor being so huge, I got a clear view of who was on the other side checking me out and giving me orders. Most of the men I dealt with were fine as fuck, but there were a few who needed to get their shit together. Like my client Blair. He was a white man who made arrangements for me to hook up with him around midnight, either every day or every other day. He was married to some ol' cockeyed bitch, and when he showed me a picture of her, I laughed and understood why he was paying his hard earned money to get off while watching me. He was kind of weird, though. There was something about his dark, sneaky eyes that I didn't necessarily like.

The good thing about Internet video porn was that nobody knew shit about me or my sisters. All they had was an Internet connection and fake-ass names that were either our pseudonyms or names that those who paid us wanted us to go by. I'd been every name from Nancy to Cookie to a nasty, freaky bitch. My pseudonym was Black Satin only because of my dark skin, and because I loved black silk.

I closed the door to my bedroom and changed into my teddy. The rule was to never interrupt each other while we were at work, unless we had a joint session where all of us were included. Those sessions were cool, but we made the men aware that none of us would be touching each other, sucking on each other, kissing each other, or no shit like that. We didn't get down like that, and all we could offer them was the display of some bumping and grinding.

I glanced at the clock on my nightstand and it showed 9:55 p.m. With my teddy on, I checked myself in the oval-shaped mirror that sat tall off the floor. I then reached in my jewelry box to find something sexy to drape around my neck. There was no question that women liked diamonds, but some men found pearls to be sexy. I wrapped several white pearls around my neck and let them fall between my firm, thick breasts. I then covered my body in a shimmering lotion that added glitter specks to my skin. I stepped into my seven-inch red heels that hiked my ass up to where it needed to be. My monitor was already on, so I relaxed in the chair in front of my desk and waited for my ten o'clock appointment to arrive.

Mr. Honey's e-mail came right on time. I logged into my account, entered my password, and after providing him with a code, there he was looking at me from the other side of my computer. His smile was wide, his body was fit, and always paying attention to eyes, they sure as hell were sexy. He was a charcoal dark-skinned nigga with locs that fell on his shoulders. I could see his muscular frame on the monitor, and as he started to talk to me, his voice was deep and smooth. I returned the smile and crossed my long legs.

He licked across his thick lips then touched the trimmed hair on his chin. "You look even sexier than your pictures are. I knew I was on to something special when I saw you," he said.

Always seducing my clients on the other side, I leaned forward to give him a peek at my cleavage as I squeezed my breasts together. I had a red sucker in my hand for teasing, and with red hot lipstick on, I knew my beauty was coming through strong for me over the screen. My long curls remained pulled to the side and rested on one shoulder. And diamond earrings dangled from my earlobes.

"I hope you like what you see, and you damn right you're on to somethin' special. But my question to you is why so much money? What exactly is it that you want me to do, and why choose me instead of some white trick who been in this business longer than me and makes a fortune?"

It was no secret to us that white women owned this profession. They did this shit in the privacy of their own homes, and walked out their doors as if they were honorable hockey and soccer moms who could do no wrong. It was a white woman who hooked Mama up on the game, and it didn't take long for none of us to learn the ropes and start making some for real money. We now had this shit on lock and it came natural for us. There was too much money to be made on this, but the average ghetto bitch couldn't pull this off. A bitch had to have skills, a near flawless body, and she had to know how to communicate with men. I didn't give a shit if the motherfucker on the other side was fine as hell or uglier than a gray goose. As long as he didn't have to touch me, and he paid for my services, I was good.

"I've had my share of white women," Honey admitted. "But I was in the mood to share my time with someone I could relate to. As for the money, I didn't think you would settle for anything less. I saw your profile and I said to myself that you would be worth every single penny."

I backed away from the screen, took several licks from the sucker then set it on my desk. One pearl went into my mouth, and as I rubbed the pearls across my lips, I narrowed my eyes and gazed at Mr. Honey.

"So, what is it that you want me to do for all of this money? You still haven't told me."

"For starters, all I want to do is get a full glimpse of you. Stand up for me. Let me see what you're workin' with."

I had no problem doing that. I moved the chair back and raised my arms in the air. My eyes scanned down my arms and moved to my breasts as I posed in different positions to entice Honey. He could see my hard nipples and butterfly-shaved pussy hairs through my sheer teddy. Adding much more to the mix, I turned around and presented my pretty ass to him. It was smooth and flawless, without any blemishes, scars, bumps; only a dimple, but nothing that made me look like plenty of bitches who tried to pull this off. My sisters and I were rare. We did whatever it took to make ourselves look good and keep our bodies in shape. The Kardashians didn't have shit on us, with the exception of more money.

With my back facing the monitor, I turned my head to the side and reached my hand around to grab my own ass. I held a chunk of it and nothing but thick meat squeezed through my fingers. Honey's eyes were zoned in. I knew I had that motherfucker hooked. I bent over, and when I spread my ass cheeks apart, he could see my juicy slit that I would stick my finger into later.

"That's enough for right now," he said. I guessed it must have been too much for him, but this wasn't shit. There was more to come.

I returned to my chair and placed my foot against my desk. My legs were open for him to get a good view of my goodies. I watched as his eyes fluttered then closed.

"What's the problem, big boy? You can't handle all of this? I thought you could, so open your eyes and let's get down to the real business."

Honey opened his eyes. He leaned closer to the monitor, puckering for a kiss. I did the kissing thing from time to time, and even though I couldn't feel a thing, whatever these motherfuckers wanted was fine with me.

I leaned forward, kissed the monitor, and planted a soft "kiss" on his lips.

"That was sweet," he said, backing away from the monitor. "I feel much better, but before we get started, do you mind if I get naked too?"

I shrugged. "Of course not. G'on ahead and do you, baby. I'll watch you from over here."

When Honey stood up, he looked hella thick. His body was ripped from his chest down. I had seen men with nice physiques but not like his. He had to be a bodybuilder or a professional athlete. He tried to tease me when he slowly removed his white boxers, but I wasn't a bitch who got overly excited about big dicks. I had seen plenty of them. From four inches to fifteen inches, my monitor displayed them all from the other side. Honey was working with about a twelve and he was proud to show it to me.

"You like that?" he said, holding his massive-sized dick in his hand.

With seduction in my eyes, I stroked his ego by licking across my lips. "Nice. Real nice. I wish I could feel it deep in my pussy. I bet it would feel so good in my pussy. What do you think?" I had to say those kinds of things just to keep the mood flowing.

"I sure would like to see, but I know you don't get down like that. You'll never meet me, or would you?"

I sucked on another one of my pearls and widened my legs just a little bit more for him to see more of me. "Never. I meet no one."

"Not even me?"

"Not even you."

"Why not?"

"The question is why should I? Because you got a big dick and some money? Please."

"So the fact that I have a big dick and money doesn't move you?"

"I'm not sayin' that it doesn't. It's movin' me so much right now that my pussy is startin' to throb as I'm thinkin' about you bein' in it. But I doubt that it can move me from this chair and outside of this room."

"Not even if I bump up the money?"

"You can bump it up all you want to. I still may not change my mind."

"We'll have to see about that. I think you can be persuaded, once we're done with this."

All I could do was smile. Every client I had thought they could pull out their dicks and get me to change my mind about meeting with them.

It wasn't going to happen, so I never focused too much time on that bullshit. I always got back to the reason they were willing to pay me for less than thirty minutes of my time. Honey had spent so much time talking that his time was about to run out on him.

I ignored what he'd said and raised myself from the chair. I stood back so he could see me and I started to remove the teddy. I eased the straps off my shoulders then rolled the top part down underneath my breasts. They plopped out making a statement and so did my nipples, which were already hard. I didn't lie when I told Honey I was turned on. The truth of the matter was, I really did love dick. But not dick that came from the other side. Only dick that came on occasion, when I was out clubbing with my sisters and I spotted a fine nigga who I wanted to fuck me. A nigga who came with no attachments and who didn't demand anything else from me. I never gave a phone number for them to call me, and every motherfucker I was with knew that it would only be a one-night stand. At least, I hoped that they knew. Since I hadn't been fucked in over a month, I gave Honey something real special. It was what I considered the red carpet treatment.

My teddy had already hit the floor. All I stood in were pearls and high heels. I swished my hips from side to side as I walked over to my bed and lay sideways across it. After tucking my body pillow between my legs, I glared at Honey who looked mesmerized on the screen.

"I would give anything to be that pillow." His dick was already in his hand and he had begun to stroke it. "Proceed, baby girl. Let me see what you got."

Talk was cheap, so I turned myself into Black Satin and got down to business. I covered myself with body oils and rubbed them all over me. My oily hands slipped into my pussy and I fucked myself into an orgasm. My sensual cries from pleasure escaped in the air and were loud enough for Honey to hear. I could hear his heavy breathing as I moved to the edge of the bed and bent over. I pretended that he was behind me, and I yelled out his name as I fingered myself and toyed with my own clit. I didn't believe that there was a bitch in this world who could fuck her own self like I could and bring about so much pleasure. I had mastered how to turn myself on, and I knew every part of my body to touch to make that happen.

Honey had already busted a nut. I heard him spill nasty shit from his mouth that kind of turned me on more. I kneeled on the bed, pretending that he was underneath me. Needless to say, I fucked the shit out of him and rode him like only a bad bitch like me could. That motherfucker cheered me on. By the time I was finished, we both were exhausted. I lay back on the bed and thought about how I was going to shortcut the rest of my clients tonight. The first one always got the best of me, but it sometimes went downhill after that. Chyna and Karrine told me that by the end of the night they felt energized. I didn't. You could only get so many orgasms out of me in one night.

"Five thousand," Honey said. "Meet me tomorrow and I'll give you five thousand dollars."

I moved my head from side to side with a grin on my face. "No can do. Why won't you listen to me, man? I already told you I don't operate like that."

"I know what you said, but I'm saying that we need to hook up. One time, that's it. You and me, and we can meet wherever you want us to. No strings attached. Once we're done, you can go your way, I'll go mine. You can't expect to fuck with my head like that and not want to give me the real deal."

I laughed and sat up on the bed. There was something about Honey that was intriguing, but

I didn't know what it was. He had me thinking about his request, but maybe it was just the money. I wanted to know how much more he was willing to give, so I rejected his first offer.

"Honey, I would love to hook up with you, but unfortunately I can't. The rules are the rules. Didn't you read them before you signed up to meet me?"

"I don't want to play by your rules though. I want you to play by my rules. I'm willing to pay any dollar amount to see if I can get that to happen."

Honey's time was running out. In less than five minutes, I had to be ready for my next client. The room was messy, my hair wasn't tight, and not to mention that I didn't have on any clothes. I had to continue this conversation with Honey some other time, but when I opened my mouth, he shouted out loudly.

"Ten thousand dollars! I'll drop it into your account right now. Let me know what's up and tell me where you want me to meet you. All I need is one, maybe two hours of yo' time."

Now this motherfucker had my attention. My mind was racing. I'd never had anybody throw ten Gs out at me and it would definitely give me bragging rights when it came to my sisters.

I had to quickly make up my mind, and without giving it much more thought, I nodded.

"Okay, Honey. I'll meet with you, but only one time. After that, I'm cuttin' you clean off. You won't be able to contact me again. Drop the money into my account, and I'll contact you through e-mail with a destination. Don't fuck me or else you gon' wish that you never signed up for this."

Honey chuckled at my words, but all I did was disconnect him from the screen. If he thought I was bullshitting with him, he'd better think again. I thought he was bullshitting with me, too, but after I got finished with my second gig for the night and checked my account, the ten Gs were there. A smirk washed over my face, and in a day or two, I'd be ready to show Mr. Honey what I was really working with.

Chapter Ten

Chyna

I had made several grand in one week, but Simone doubled my shit in one day. As we sat around in the living room watching TV, she counted her money out loudly. Her feet were propped on the table and a wide grin was plastered on her face.

"What you bitches got to say about that?" she said, slamming the money on the table. "Who said that I was the lowest payin' bitch here?"

We all laughed. Karrine and I had to renege on all the negative shit we'd said to Simone about her not bringing in enough money.

"You just lucked up on that nigga," I said. "But good for you. I'm just not sure if you should meet him. The last time one of us rushed out of here to do that, y'all know what happened."

"Well, it won't happen like that again. This time, we all know better."

Karrine had tripped the last time. She actually made the mistake of meeting that fool at his house and the wife came in on them. The wife tried to stab the shit out of Karrine, but when the wife couldn't catch her, she turned her anger toward her husband. She sliced his ass up and Karrine got the fuck out of there. She called us from a payphone to come get her, and when we picked her up, she was hysterical. That's when Mama made a rule that we were not to go visit anyone, no matter how much they were willing to pay. It didn't mean that we followed her rule about that, and whenever we did do something on the side, we kept it among each other. Mama didn't know anything, and there wasn't no chance of her finding out because none of us were snitching.

"So, when you gon' meet him?" Karrine asked. "Today, tomorrow, when?"

"Today. He's been waitin' patiently for me. I got another e-mail from him yesterday, asking if I'd made up my mind about where to meet."

"Have you?" I asked.

"Yep. I'ma meet him at a motel downtown. Ain't no need for all that fancy shit, especially when I'm only goin' there to do what I do."

Simone stood and tugged on the red minidress she wore. She had on a black off-the-shoulder top that was cut above her midriff. She looked ready to go, and said that once she got on her shoes, she'd be ready to go do her thing.

"Be sure to write down the motel address, room number, and phone number so we can have that information. And once you're in there, be sure to call and let us know," I said.

Simone said she would, and as she got ready to go, Karrine and I stayed in the living room talking and watching TV. Mama had been gone since the other day. She called to let us know she was okay, and when I heard a slot machine in the background, I figured she had to be somewhere gambling.

She was probably at the local casino, where she, sometimes, stayed many nights. But that's how Mama got down. She enjoyed her life to the fullest, as we all did, but the plan was to move out of Chicago and buy a mansion somewhere near the sandy beaches in Florida or Cali.

Moving to Florida or Cali was our dream, but we had been splurging on so much of the money that we could never seem to save enough to see our dream through. We could've taken the money from Ray's bank account to go toward our dream home, but instead we used the money for other things. It took a lot to keep ourselves as beautified as we were, and it wasn't like we wanted to live like broke ghetto hoes or drive around in cars that broke down on the road whenever we had someplace to be. We desired to live the high life, and until we decided to make some for real sacrifices, the townhouse we resided in had to do.

Simone gave us the info on where she would be. She left and I waited for her to send a text message saying that she had come face to face with her money man.

Almost forty-five minutes later, the text came across. Karrine and I swooped up our purses to go. We rode to the motel in her gold Mercedes. Mama had the Range Rover and Simone had the Bentley. I wondered how strange it probably looked parked outside of a sleazy motel. Then again, motel parking lots had been the place where you could find many expensive cars parked.

"Do you know where this place is?" Karrine asked while behind the steering wheel.

"I think I do, but pull over at the gas station to get some gas. Your car is almost on empty."

Karrine pulled over to a BP gas station that was packed with niggas hanging out. A drunk nigga with a liquor bottle tightened with a brown paper bag stood by the door, begging for change. I walked right by him with my tight pink shorts on and colorful baby doll top. I was the vibrant sister. The one who liked to add color to myself, especially since I was already dark. The color black did nothing whatsoever for me, and I loved loud colors that always drew attention to me. The men checked me out as if I were prey. Lips were licking, throats were clearing, and plenty men were grabbing their nuts. I knew I was a bad bitch, but I used my good looks and sexy body in the way Mama had taught me to use it. Nothing was for free and dick wasn't good for nothing but getting my pussy wet. I had learned how to do that myself, but like my other sisters, from time to time, a real dick was needed. None, however, was at the gas station, so I ignored the whistles and hollas as I went into the store and paid for Karrine to fill her tank. When I walked out, I dropped a penny in the begging man's hand.

"If you got money for that liquor, and a hand to hold it, get yo' ass a job, nigga. Stop beggin' people for they shit and don't blow yo' stank breath on me again."

The man's fire red eyes damn near broke from their sockets. He was shocked by what I'd said to him and two niggas who stood close by were laughing their asses off. I walked up to Karrine and gave her a soda while she pumped the gas. All eyes were definitely on us, and one of the dudes who was laughing came up to the car. As I got a closer look at him, he was fine as fuck. Had a bit of swag going on, so I didn't necessarily trip when he stepped to me.

"You was kind of rude to that old man, wasn't you?" Dude sucked his teeth and grinned at me with a mouth full of gold. His sagging jeans hung low, and with the oversized T-shirt on, I couldn't tell if his body was hooked up. His hazel eyes, though, were sexy as shit.

"Why you all up in my business and not mindin' your own?" I asked.

"You expect for me to mind my business with you and yo' friend standin' here lookin' this damn good? That ain't happenin', ma, not today."

Karrine didn't have time for small talk like I sometimes did. Plus we had business to tend to. Dude was holding us up.

"Thanks for the compliment, but I need to make a move. Maybe some other time."

"Some other time like tonight?" He gave me a business card. "Call me if you gamin'. Now all you have to do is tell me your name so I'll know it's you."

I leaned forward and whispered in dude's ear. "Shame," I said. "My name is Shame."

He cocked his head back. "Shame? Why in the fuck yo' mama name you Shame? That's messed up."

"She didn't name me Shame, but I'm tellin' you that it's a shame that I'm not goin' to use your number. Why? Because you got another bitch sittin' in yo' car, eyeing me down like I'm the one who done somethin' to her. She should be mad at your disrespectful ass, so get the fuck away from me before I spit in your face."

The nigga quickly backed up. He had a smirk on his face when he went back over to his car trying to explain to his woman that he knew me from school. I hated niggas who thought they could get away with that kind of bullshit. And I also despised women more who played into the hands of niggas like that. Know when to say no and keep it the fuck moving. If a motherfucker was bold enough to dis his woman like that, he'd do the same to the next bitch.

I got back in the car, strapped my seat belt across me, and held on tight as Karrine breezed through traffic and made it to the motel. By now it was almost 8:00 p.m. We were sure that Simone had to be fucking her money man by then. We arrived at the motel and Karrine parked her car next to Simone's. We both took deep breaths, and never quite knowing what we would walk in on in situations like this, we came ready.

This wasn't the first time we did something like this and it wouldn't be the last. For fools who were willing to pay as much as Honey had, we saw those niggas as weak. Weak minds that would do anything for pussy. We also figured these fools had more paper somewhere, so we plotted and put up a little more effort to get it. Even if that meant offering real pussy, that's what we did. In no way would the men be pleased with us once we were finished. They would either be down some additional cash in their bank accounts or they would leave with their pockets completely empty.

Wearing minimal disguises, all I did while in the car was change my hair up by putting my long braids into a ponytail. I also put a baseball cap on my head. Karrine covered her head with a doo-rag and she wore baggy clothes so you couldn't see her shapely figure. Simone said that the door to room 112 would be unlocked, and as soon as we busted through the door, we could see her riding the shit out of the man who went by the name of Honey. Simone jerked her head around, and Honey lifted his head to look over her shoulder. His hands were gripped on her ass, and he'd had one of her breasts in his mouth, sucking the shit out of it. To my surprise, he was fine as fuck! I damn sure loved a nigga with locs flowing down to his shoulders.

Simone touched Honey's chest that was already heaving in and out. He didn't dare open his mouth, especially not with two Glock 9s aiming directly at his head.

"Damn, baby," Simone said, raising herself off his dick. "I was just gettin' ready to get mine. It looks like that ain't gon' happen."

She slithered her naked body against his until she was down by his dick. He took a deep breath when she sucked it into her mouth and she moaned while doing it.

"Wha . . . what's goin' on?" he asked without stopping her.

His question was directed to me and Karrine, as we ransacked the room, searching for credit cards and money. He had three credit cards in his wallet and a debit card from Bank of America. I walked up to the bed and placed the gun on his temple.

"PIN to your debit card," I said.

"Mmmmmm," Simone moaned while still sucking his stick. She deep throated him, causing his body to jerk.

"Five. Nine. One. Seven," he said. "Now why—"

"No questions. I promise that we won't hurt you, especially not if you cooperate."

Karrine wrote down the number and listened for the PINs for the rest of his cards.

"Credit card limits on each card, startin' with the Visa."

He didn't respond, so Simone stepped it up. She kept a smile on her face while inserting his dick back into her. As she started to grind on him, he spoke up.

"A . . . about seven thousand on the Visa and a combination of fifty thousand on the other two."

Karrine took notes again. Simone, however, was about to hit a homerun.

"Shit this dick is good!" she shouted. "I wish you would work with me on this because my pussy is tinglin' so bad! All it needs is a little more movement inside of it."

Mr. Honey was so upset that he wouldn't even be a sport and participate in the festivities. He sat still with a mean mug on his face that left not one of us nervous.

"I have your driver's license," I said, waving it in his face. "I have your wife's social security number and I know where she works. I also know where you live, so don't try nothin' stupid."

There was a business card in his wallet with that info, so I figured since they had the same last name, the woman was his wife. I also had a picture of her skinny ass and all I could do was frown.

"This is really an ugly bitch," I said, looking down at the pictures. "As fine as you are, can't yo' ass do better than this?"

Karrine came closer to look at the picture of the frail-looking woman with blond hair and green eyes. And when I showed it to Simone, she stopped riding him.

"You mean to tell me that I've been givin' you all this good pussy and yo' dick been in somethin' like that? Man, I'm done with this. I don't even want or need an orgasm."

She lifted herself off of him, and it was so funny because the nigga's dick was still hard. He made a move to sit up on his elbows while still lying on the bed. Karrine positioned her gun at him and told him to be still.

Simone wiped her wet pussy with the sheet then tossed it back on the bed. She hurried to put her shirt and skirt back on then stepped into her shoes.

"We're almost done here, but here's the deal: if you call the police, people may have to start dyin' and you may not like that. If you call your credit card companies, people may have to start dyin' and you may not like that. Your kids and wife will start to learn shit about you that they didn't know, but if you keep yo' mouth shut, all of this goes away. You'll be embarrassed behind this, but you'll eventually get over it. All I can say is don't make the mistake of lettin' this happen again, and the next time a chick says she don't want to hook up with you, just let her be."

Honey hadn't moved, but he looked to understand and to be cooperative. We headed for the door and his words stopped us in our tracks.

"You know y'all gon' pay for this shit, right?" he said.

We all looked at each other and rolled our eyes in different directions. Karrine lifted her gun and without hesitating she pulled the trigger. The bullet whistled through the air and went into the wall behind him where the bathroom was on the other side. Glass shattered, and all Honey did was duck and hold his trembling hands close to his head.

"No, nigga, you gon' pay," I said. "Not us."

We left and peeled off the parking lot so quickly that if you blinked you missed us. Karrine and I laughed about what had happened with Mr. Money Man, and before we went home, we stopped at an ATM to withdraw $1,000 from each of his accounts, which was the one-day maximum. We had plans to do some shopping later, but as soon as we got home, Mama was sitting on the round, micro-fabric linen sofa in the living room with her legs crossed. Her arms rested on top of the couch and trouble was lurking behind her eyes as she peered at us near the doorway.

"Did y'all enjoy yourselves today?" she asked, then moved her eyes to the nine millimeter that was resting peacefully on the table in front of her.

"We had a great time today," Karrine said, always the first one to answer Mama when we could tell there would be trouble.

Mama eased up from the couch then picked up the gun. "How great?" she said step by step, making her way up to us.

By now, we were all looking at each other. There wasn't no way in hell that Mama had known what we'd done because we knew it wouldn't be in our best interest to snitch on each other. The only way she could have found out what went down today was if that motherfucker, himself, had told her.

Then again, maybe Mama was just trying to feel us out. She damn sure wasn't about to blow our goddamn brains out, so I wasn't sure why she was fronting with the gun. She did look mad, though, so maybe it was smart for us to come clean.

Mama stood in front of us without a blink. Since Simone had come in, it was now three to one. We could definitely take her, if we wanted to. But Mama had done too much shit for us to play her like that. She went to hell and back for us and taught us things about life that so many mothers had failed to do with their daughters. It wasn't like she had ever abandoned us or anything, or that she was some crackhead-ass mama who left her kids in the hands of other people. So it was our bad if we lied to her on occasion about doing crazy shit behind her back. We knew she'd come down on our heads if we ever got caught up into some shit we ain't have no business doing. Maybe today was the day that we all had to face what we had done and deal with the backlash of it all.

Mama patted the nine millimeter against her leg and tapped her foot on the floor. She stared into my eyes first, and when I looked away, her eyes shifted to Karrine's. They didn't stop there and landed on Simone. She lowered her head, and when Mama reached out her hand, Simone jerked her head back. All Mama did was touch her chin and lift it.

"Tell me what happened, baby," Mama said in a soft voice but with no expression on her face.

"Wha . . . what happened with what, Mama?" Simone said.

"I'm goin' to ask you again. Tell me what happened, and do not lie to me. Remember the rules around here? No lies, and no love, unless the love is for each other. Remember?"

Simone nodded. We were all nervous. I hoped like hell that Simone just went ahead and told Mama the truth. She obviously knew what had happened. How? I didn't know yet. It didn't make sense to try to figure out how she'd found out. Time was running out, and the truth needed to be spoken. Simone attempted to tackle it first.

"I remember, so here's the truth. You recall that man, Honey, who I told you about? Well, he paid me ten Gs to meet him and have sex with him. I agreed to do it, and I just left the motel where we were. After havin' sex with him, I robbed him. Took his money and credit cards and threatened to tell his wife and shame his name if he told anyone. I know you're against me doin' shit like that, but I saw it as a good opportunity for me to make some more paper. All I was tryin' to do was fill my pockets with more paper."

Once Simone was done spilling her guts to Mama, she caught us all off guard when she lifted her hand and slapped Simone across the face with the nine millimeter. Simone hit the floor, hard. I gasped loudly and Karrine's hands started to shake. The cracking sound that the gun made against Simone's jaw took every breath out of me. She held her face and squeezed her eyes together. Mama damn sure didn't raise no punks, but what she had done to Simone was considered out of line. Even if it was the partial truth, Mama didn't seem to care.

Her face scrunched as she looked from one of us to the other. "Do y'all think I'm a goddamn fool? Is that what y'all think? What have I done, as a mother, to make you heifers deceive me like y'all did today? Are y'all that fuckin' stupid to believe that I don't know what the fuck y'all have been up to? Well, I do know, and I'm about to change the rules around here until y'all realize who the real bitch in charge around here is."

Mama looked down at Simone. "Get the fuck up," she said. "And neither of y'all betta not shed no tears, 'cause if you do, I'ma fuck somebody up again. Mr. Honey was used as a pawn. I had him set yo' ass up, Simone, just to see if you would be stupid enough to leave this house and take your trashy tail somewhere and fuck somebody for cash. I had no idea," Mama said, and looked at Karrine then at me, "that the two of you would run up into that motel room, doing some Bonnie and Clyde bullshit and rob Honey." Then Mama lifted her other hand that wasn't holding the gun and slapped the shit out of Karrine. Slapped her so hard that if she'd had any hair on her head, it would've converted it into another style.

Karrine bit down on her lip and glared at Mama behind her narrowed eyes. Mama was already hyped about the other day, so she walked over and stood face to face with Karrine. "Then you had the nerve to pull the trigger and shoot at the motherfucker. Are you a murderer now? Is that what you want to be, Karrine? If you do, tell me now so I can gather all of my precious money that I've made over the years to bail your ass out of jail! Do you want to go to jail?" Spit speckles from Mama's mouth dotted Karrine's face. When she reached up to wipe them, Mama snatched Karrine's hands away from her face. "Answer me, damn it! Do you?"

All Karrine did was move her head from side to side.

"I didn't think so, 'cause jail ain't where yo' black ass wanna be. I've been there already. I know how them bitches get down and it damn sure ain't no picnic. So listen up, ladies."

Mama stepped back and gave Karrine some breathing room. Her face was still scrunched as she pointed her finger and made her demands.

"Since you bitches think y'all can go around lying to me, the rules will have to change. First off, Honey wants his shit back and, Simone, you gon' have to be the brave, bad bitch you want to be and take all of his shit back to him. He's not too happy about what y'all did, and if he puts his foot in yo' ass, don't come crying back to me. Next, any and all niggas who reach out to y'all on the Internet need to be approved by me. I need access to your bank accounts, and every transaction I need to know who made it and when. There will be no more freedom to do as you wish around here and your money will be put on hold until I feel satisfied enough to give it to you. If y'all want me to treat y'all like I'm a pimp then I fucking will. Lastly, whenever you leave this house, I need to know your whereabouts. There will be no more running in and out of here as you please. If you don't like my new rules, you can always get the hell out. If you make that choice, y'all will never be able to bring y'all asses back here again."

I was a grown-ass woman. I didn't appreciate the kind of game Mama was playing. That shit wouldn't stick, and by the looks on Karrine's and Simone's faces, I could tell it wasn't going to fly with them either. Yeah, we had made a mistake, a big mistake, by going up into that motel room and robbing that nigga, but it's what we did. Mama knew what kind of women we were, and I didn't get why she was tripping so hard with this nigga Honey. Who exactly was he to her, and why in the fuck would she set up Simone like that anyway?

Mama started to walk away, leaving us confused, angry, and plotting at the same time. She turned before she reached the staircase and halted her steps.

"For the record," she said, "I'm the only motherfucker on this earth who can and will hurt you. It can be that way sometimes and that's what mothers do, especially when their children get out of line. Y'all put yourselves in a position today that could have costs y'all yo' lives. Don't ever do that shit again because there will be consequences for fucking up, especially when you don't have to. Y'all bitches got it made here, so think before you act next time. That way, Simone, you won't wind up with your own brother's dick in your mouth and slobbering all over his balls. Honey is Ray's youngest son, but had you been honest with me from jump, I could have told you that. Your mistake, not mine."

Simone held her stomach and rushed off to the bathroom. I stood like electricity had shocked me and Karrine's eyes were so wide that they almost popped out of her head. Mama made her way up the steps, swaying her hips from left to right. She often told us that when you know better you do better. I had hoped so, but there was never any question that my sisters and I always kept ourselves in hella trouble. There was a lot of shit that Mama didn't know about, but if or when she found out, just like today, I expected for the shit to hit the fan.

Chapter Eleven

Simone

I had slipped once, fell twice, and bumped my damn head on the floor. When Mama told me that I had fucked my own brother, I almost died. Then, I had the nerve to put his dick inside of my mouth, too. That was downright fucked up. I wondered why she didn't just tell me that Honey was my brother from jump. It didn't make sense for Mama to set me up, just to see if I made moves with the niggas I'd been enticing through video porn. The last motherfucker I went to see in person, his name was Blake. I kind of liked him, but that didn't stop me from robbing him. That little job was handled by me, alone, and I left my sisters out of it. I didn't want them always involved with my dirty work, and I was afraid that they'd tell Mama about how I really got down. It was all about making paper for me, and there was a part of me that was upset because Chyna and Karrine always made more than I did. I mean, video porn took care of us, no doubt, but lining my pockets with paper didn't always stop there for me.

As the baby girl, I had to go the extra mile to get more money any way that I could. I loved that niggas couldn't just have easy access to my body, and the only way they could get to me was by looking at their computer monitors. Or, if I broke the rules and went to meet them. Like I said, that was rare. But if I did meet somebody in person, most likely, they would wind up being one of my victims.

There was no question about it that I loved my sisters and Mama, but some things were left better off not said. I didn't care to share that I'd been fucking this dude named Reno, but he kept putting our business out in the streets. I didn't like it. If my sisters had heard about me hooking up with Reno then I knew he'd been making a lot of noise. I told Chyna and Karrine that Reno was a goddamn liar and I left it at that.

I also told Reno to keep his fucking mouth shut about us, or else I would cut off his balls and shove them in his mouth. He thought I was playing, but I guessed he didn't know me as well as he'd thought. He promised me that he wouldn't say another word to anyone, but I didn't trust him for nothing in the world. The bottom line was there were consequences for niggas who bragged about getting a piece of this pussy and who didn't know when to shut the fuck up. He would never, ever touch me again, and if I could somehow or someway get away with it, I'd shove a Glock in his mouth and silence that nigga for good.

The only other issues I'd had, aside from this new thing with Honey, was from Blake. He used to be a regular. He had been trying to reach me through e-mails for months. He questioned why I'd played him and took $4,000 from his bank account, but that was the easy part. It was like taking candy from a baby that day, and he was mesmerized by my pussy. I seriously put it on him, and as he fell asleep in the hotel room, I took his wallet, stole his checkbook, and wrote myself a fat-ass check that I cashed later that day. I was a little nervous at the bank, but once the cash was in my hand, I was good. I was a risk-taker for sure, and unlike Karrine and Chyna, there were times when I got a thrill out of doing shit like that. It made me feel powerful, and just like my Mama, I loved living on the edge. I hated thirsty-ass niggas, and men like Blake simply deserved what they got.

He didn't come out of the coma he was in until the next day, and by that time, the damage had been done. I disappeared, and every time he attempted to reach out to me through e-mails, I deleted them. After a while, I never heard from him again.

That was over four months ago, but as I sat in front of my computer, polishing my toenails red and waiting for my nine o'clock appointment to login, I got an e-mail from Blake, asking if I would respond to him.

Please, Black Satin. I thought we had a connection. If money is what you wanted, all you had to do was ask. I would have given it to you.

I decided to fuck with Blake. I was already in a bad mood from Mama slapping the shit out of me with a gun earlier, and I wasn't looking forward to meeting with my so-called brother, Honey, to return the money and credit cards we had stolen from him. Mama said I had to do it or else. I put my visit to Honey on the schedule for first thing in the morning, and hopefully, by then, he wouldn't be too hot with me for setting his ass up. I figured Chyna or Karrine wouldn't go with me, but I hoped that their night in front of the monitor was going better than mine.

Karrine had a bruise on her face from Mama smacking her, and I suspected that her clients would ask her what had happened. I had a mark on my face too, but after a few dabs of makeup, the bruise was covered up. If anybody just happened to see it and ask what had happened, my response would be that it was none of their business. Chyna was the only one who Mama hadn't laid her hands on, but that wasn't no surprise to us. It would take a lot for Mama to go there with her. It was no secret that Chyna was Mama's favorite.

Chyna had gone to her room around eight o'clock to do her thing, but she seemed upset about Mama's new rules too. Pertaining to her rules, I doubted that any of us would turn our money over to her; I doubted that we would let her know our whereabouts and I doubted that we would seek her approval for the men we connected with through video porn.

Yeah, she was upset about what we'd done, but one goddamn mistake could be forgiven. I was so glad that she was in her bedroom, resting well. Or, at least, I hoped she was.

I replied to Blake:

Stop beggin'. I hate a man who begs, and you need to know that there was no connection. I liked you and all, but I liked your money more. Sorry for the mishap, but you'll have to get over it. Bye.

Blake didn't respond, but minutes later, pretty boy Antonio had logged in and was ready to take a thirty-minute adventure with me. I only charged him $750, because he was a young college student who was getting money from his rich parents. The money was supposed to be spent on books, but he had some serious desires for little ol' me. I loved to toy with him and seeing his sexiness on my monitor always got me hyped about what I was doing.

"What's going on today in your world, sexy?" he asked. Antonio raked his fingers through his wild, curly hair. His thick brows and bronze-colored skin made him look Mexican, but his parents were mixed.

"It's all good, but much better now that you're here."

Antonio blushed. I knew most of my clients well, and I had learned what to say and what not to say to them. I could tell when they were in shitty moods and needed me to go the extra mile for them, or when they were in good moods and were satisfied with whatever I dished out for the day.

Antonio was in that kind of mood. His favorite thing to watch was me playing with my pussy. I had a ten-inch, deep black dildo that I inserted into me. He loved to see me fuck myself with it.

Antonio didn't talk a lot, but he talked enough. He didn't have to tell me when he was ready for his sexual journey to begin, because I always knew it. His dick would always be in his hand, with Vaseline nearby.

Dressed in a red sheer baby doll negligee and string-tied panties, I stood and exposed my near nakedness on the screen. On Antonio's end, I was sure he could see my hard nipples poking through the sheer fabric of my negligee, and the crotch of my panties were sucked in by my shaved pussy lips. I moved closer to the screen and pulled the crotch section of my panties aside. I dipped two of my fingers inside of me then released a gasping moan into the air, loud enough for him to hear me.

"I want to taste you so badly," he said softly. "I swear your pussy looks good enough to eat. I wish I could have it for dinner."

"You can have me for breakfast, lunch, dinner, and for a snack. Just make an appointment."

Antonio laughed, and speaking the truth, so did I.

With my fingers still deep inside of me, I turned around and displayed my round, near perfect ass to him. There was a small dimple on my right cheek that he loved, and he always mentioned it. I think he was the only client of mine who knew my body inside out. He noticed when I had gotten a tattoo on my wrist that read FIERCE and he noticed the rose near my ankle. When I had my coochie hairs shaved into the shape of a butterfly, he noticed that, too. I bent far over, knowing that he could clearly see my fingers play on my pussy like a violin. It wasn't long before my pussy started to rain and heavy glaze iced my fingers.

"I swear I'm about to have a heart attack over here," he said.

I looked back at the monitor, seeing that his eyes were wide open. He was so focused on what I was doing that he'd let go of his dick, just to watch my performance. It thrilled me to death to be able to excite niggas in such a way. Antonio looked high as fuck and he wasn't coming off that high anytime soon.

Since he was so into it, I brought out the big guns. Well, that meant my big black smooth dilly that I couldn't wait to put into me. It had suction on the bottom, so I was able to prop it up wherever I wanted to. I chose a sidebar on my desk, just so I could turn at the appropriate angle for Antonio to scope the dick sliding in and out of me.

"If you gon' have a heart attack, maybe I need to quit now. Are you sure you can handle this?"

He rushed to speak up. "Yeah, yeah, I can. Go ahead and make it good. Make it real good for me, okay? I need this. My finals are stressing me. You have no idea how much of a stress reliever you are."

Hell, yes, I knew it. I'd heard that a lot. It was my duty to make sure my clients exited my world relieved of their stress. I touched the head of the dildo and massaged it with K-Y Jelly. I then backed up to it and felt pressure as it parted my pussy lips and spread me wide open. I was already dripping wet from my finger-fucking festivities, but I got even more soaked when I started to back my ass up on the dildo and work it.

It felt like the real deal, so I tightened my eyes and tickled my cherry drop with my thumb. Without looking at Antonio, I could hear his heavy breathing. I knew his dick was now in his hands, so I kept moaning for him to fuck me.

"Mmmm," I said while licking across my lips. "Get it all in there, Antonio. Slide that dick in there and fuck me hard. Fuck it, baby. Damn, yo'

dick is so guuud. I can feel that shit tearin' this
pussy up."

Unfortunately, he wasn't working with much,
but I didn't have the guts to insult a paying
customer. He was only about six inches and
that was pushing it. The size of his dick in no
way mattered to me, because my big black boy
was handling his business. So much so that I
had to pull him out of me and prop him up in
the chair. I opened my legs wide and slowly
inched my way down on it. The suction held the
dick in place, while I used the arms of the chair
for leverage and rode the fuck out of the dilly as
if it belonged to a real nigga sitting in the chair.

With my legs wide open, Antonio could see
the dick going in and out of me. He could see my
heavy glaze dripping down on it, and was turned
the hell on by my dirty talk that made him stand
up and shoot his sperm directly at the monitor.
Again, I didn't give a fuck because he was the
one who had to clean that shit up. But seeing
how excited he was caused me to fake an orgasm.

"Daaaaamn, Antonio, baaaaby, that dick felt
soooo good in my pussy! This pussy is yours,
baby, all yours and let me know when you want
to fuuuuck again. You know I'll be ready!"

With an exhausted look on his face, he plopped
back in his chair. Sweat covered his forehead

and his chest heaved in and out. He was out of breath, but I surely didn't know why. That lazy motherfucker hadn't done a thing. I was the one who had done all of the work.

I removed myself from the dildo and teased him more by sucking on it. I thought about how I was going to have to up his price because $750 wasn't enough. I had been too nice to some of these horny motherfuckers. That was why Chyna and Karrine probably made more money than I did.

"You are sooo good to me," he said with his eyes closed. "I don't think I've ever had a chick be this good to me."

With the size of his dick, I wasn't sure any chick would claim the same about him. I didn't dare say that either, because I didn't want to fuck up my money. He was one of my regulars, so it was in my best interest to keep him happy. All I did was smile and sit back in the chair with my legs wide open. I rubbed my pretty pussy, which was a for real moneymaker. I took care of it, too, and I minimized the real dicks that I allowed to go into it. Antonio would never get a real feel of it, and since his thirty minutes was almost up, I leaned forward and pressed my red glossy lips against the screen. There was a time when I'd thought about robbing him too, but he was a college student. And even though his parents had money, he didn't. I wasn't going to waste my time meeting up with him, and I definitely knew who my suckers were.

"Muuuah," I said, puckering at him. "That's for you, handsome. Until next time, be good."

He nodded. I clicked the X button to shut down the video, and in an instant, he was gone. *Thank God.*

Chapter Twelve

Karrine

I had turned my tricks for the night and my bank account was sitting prettier. The redness near my eye from Mama's smack had no effect on my performances tonight, and I was able to cover the mark with makeup. With having light skin that was hard to do, but I had no worries. The men loved me, but never as much as I loved what their money did for my pockets.

It was no secret that my sisters and I were money-hungry bitches, but that was a decent title to have. We respected and accepted our profession, and not too many people knew what we had been doing behind closed doors.

Mama made that rule clear as day, but the rules that she had tossed our way wouldn't be abided by. If I wanted a pimp, I'd go get one. It was bad enough that she slapped me for shooting at Honey, but I didn't trip because we had fucked up by robbing him in the first place.

Now that the cat was out of the bag, Honey looked just like Ray. It was foolish of us not to recognize that the moment we set eyes on him. I regretted that Simone had to go take the shit we'd stolen back to him, and when she came into my room, I asked how she felt about doing it. Chyna was still in her room entertaining. I predicted that she would be done soon.

"I feel like shit," Simone said, lying back on my bed and looking up at the ceiling. "I don't even know what I'm gon' say, and I hope that nigga don't trip with me. He seemed calm when we were robbin' his ass, so I'ma just throw that shit at him and run."

We laughed then looked at the door when Chyna came in. She had on a hot-pink silk robe that cut right underneath her coochie. Her long braids hung on one shoulder and her tall, color-ful heels looked as if they were embedded with diamonds. With a round, glowing face, Chyna's beauty couldn't be touched. I could tell by the smile on her face that tonight was a good night for her.

"Almost four Gs," she said, rubbing the tips of her fingers together. "And I'm still countin'."

"You're not done yet?" Simone said. "It's almost four in the mornin'. You should be done by now."

Chyna sat on my high-heeled shoe chair that was covered in gold fabric. She crossed her legs and looked at me and Simone as we sat on the bed.

"I'm done, but Preston's cute self held me up tonight. He made me put in a little overtime. Now he wants to know if the three of us will hook up with him tonight or tomorrow. So, make the call, *chicas*. Are y'all gamin' for tonight or tomorrow? Y'all know that nigga pays up, so make the call so I can go tell him what's up."

"Tomorrow," Simone said. "We'll hook him up tomorrow. I got too much shit on my mind right now, and you know I'm hot about goin' to see Honey's ass."

"I know," Chyna said. "I'll go tell Preston to be ready tomorrow, but don't let meetin' with Honey scare you. If you want, I'll go with you. If he trip, brother or no brother, his ass can still get smoked."

"I second that shit," I said, folding my arms. "Do you want us to go with you?"

"Mama told me to go alone, and let's all get somethin' straight right now. I'm not scared of that nigga not one bit. I just don't want to confront his ass after stealin' his shit. That's all."

"And you won't have to confront him alone because we were all in that shit together," I said. "I know what Mama said, but I'm goin' with you. Chyna, you can stay here and find out where the fuck we gon' stay when we go to Vegas. I'm ready for our trip, like right now. I wish we could leave tomorrow."

"In two weeks, we're out of here," Chyna said. "I think I have an idea where I want to stay, but I'll let y'all know what's up. Until then, you go with Simone. And don't y'all get into no shit we can't get out of."

"Never," I said and we all laughed.

Early the next morning, Simone and I stood outside of what was supposed to be Honey's palace, and we knocked. It was a bad-ass, two-story crib made of brick. It had bay windows, a well-manicured lawn, big white columns, and a wrought-iron bench on the porch. Blooming flowers were everywhere, and richness was in the air. If I didn't know any better, I would've thought that some old-ass white people lived here. While Simone stood biting her nails, I knocked on the door again.

"Would you stop that?" I said to her. "I hate when you bite yo' nails like that. Besides, I thought you weren't nervous."

She spat the nail from her mouth and shot it at me. "Don't play, heifer," I said. "You better quit doin' that shit."

She playfully rolled her eyes, and then we both got serious when we saw that ugly woman whose driver's license was in Honey's wallet when we stole it. Simone thought she was his wife, but as we got a close-up look at her, that couldn't even be possible because the bitch was too damn ugly. She had a face full of potholes, her hair was a dirty blond, and she looked like she had been doing meth for ages. Her cheeks were sunk in and her beady eyes made her look evil.

"Is Honey here?" I asked.

Without saying a word, she widened the door and let us come inside. I immediately looked up at the twelve-foot ceiling and the huge crystal chandelier that hung over the marble-topped foyer. The house looked fit for a king, and I wondered where in the fuck Honey had gotten this kind of money from. Brother or no brother, this motherfucker had the hookup. Simone's eyes roamed around too, and when the scary-looking trick walked us to a nearby office, she told us to have a seat.

We sat on a leather sofa with our legs crossed. I wore gold leather pants that almost matched the blond color in my short haircut. A leopard-print, off-the-shoulder top stretched across my breasts and my stripper-like high heels made me look as if I needed to find a pole.

Simone went nowhere without red on, but the stretch mini she wore was striped with black. Her long hair had tight flowing curls in it, and a few tresses dangled near her slanted eyes.

We didn't come here to fight with Honey, but his ass needed to hurry up before I dropped his shit on the big oak desk to the right of us and left.

I looked around at the fucked-up antique-looking pictures on the walls, and at a bookshelf filled with what looked to be ancient books on it. I couldn't help but laugh, because a nigga like him didn't even read. All of this mahogany wood bullshit was for show. A world globe sat next to his desk, and wanting to spin it, I got up to do it. But as soon as I stood, Honey swooped around the corner, stopping me dead in my tracks. All he had on was a wife beater, sagging blue jeans, and Tims. His locs were pulled back into a ponytail and a small diamond glistened in his ear. There was a Rick Ross–looking motherfucking behind him. They both stood in front of us with their arms locked across their chests.

"Stand up," Honey said, looking at Simone.

I was already standing, and I damn sure didn't appreciate his tone. Neither did Simone.

"Stand up for what?" she shouted. "I'm perfectly fine sittin' right where I am. Whatever you have to say, say it so we can give you your stuff and get the fuck out of here."

Honey reached behind him and retrieved a Glock 9 from his sagging jeans. He laid it on the desk then rubbed his hands together. "Bitch, I'm not gon' repeat myself. Stand the fuck up before this shit gets ugly. I got permission from yo' mama to put my foot in yo' smart ass. I just may decide to do it."

Mama was tripping; then again, so was Honey. But in an effort to settle this shit, I asked Simone to stand and cooperate. She rolled her eyes, and after she stood up, the big motherfucker started patting us down. He started with me, but it felt like his fat ass was groping me instead of looking for something. I grabbed his hand and dug my nails deep into his flesh.

"Motherfucka, don't touch on me like that. What the fuck you lookin' for? Some available pussy? Sorry, but mine ain't available."

"Neither is mine," Simone said with her lips poked out. She smacked on her gum and dared the fat motherfucker to touch her.

Honey looked at the big nigga who had anger washed across his face. He wasn't looking too happy, and when Honey's fist tightened and slammed into Simone's midsection, that shit got my attention. She doubled over and grabbed her stomach. Honey grabbed the back of her hair and yanked her head up so she could look at him. By then, I had rushed forward, but was stopped by the big nigga who twisted my arm behind my back.

"Let me the fuck go," I shouted and released a gob of spit in his face. He didn't flinch. His grip got tighter. It was hurting so bad that I had to drop down to my knees.

"Be still," he shouted. "I swear I will break yo' goddamn arm if you keep resistin' me."

Simone's eyes were flooded with anger as she stared at Honey. Her lips were still poked out and her breathing was heavy. I couldn't remember a day or time when I saw her look so upset. Honey's actions definitely had us speechless.

"Now that I have you bitches' attention," he said. "That shit y'all did to me was foul. If I wasn't as cool as I was with Taffy, I swear I would kill both of y'all asses right now and sink you hoes in Mississippi River. But I'ma be real nice today. All I want y'all to do is give my shit back to me, get the fuck out of here, and I don't want to hear from y'all again."

"That's what we came to do," Simone said. "So let go of my goddamn hair and—"

"I swear I hate a bitch with too much mouth," he said, pulling her hair tighter. Simone squeezed her eyes, trying her best to ease the excruciating pain he was delivering. "I'm tryin' to be nice, but yo' ass won't settle for my niceness. That's too fuckin' bad because I thought you were much smarter than that, sis."

With a twisted face, he wrapped his hand around Simone's hair and dragged her over to his desk. He slammed her head on top of it and held her face with his hand so she couldn't move. He then picked up his Glock and pressed it with force against her temple. All Simone did was stare straight ahead. She said not one word, but the way she bit into her lip told me she was plotting. I tried to rush up from the floor again, but this time, I felt more pain when that big nigga tugged at my arm. All I could do on my knees was silently pray that Honey wouldn't hurt Simone and that we would be set free.

"You think yo' ass tough, don't you?" Honey said to Simone as he bent over her and whispered in her ear. She didn't answer, so he slammed the

Glock on his desk to startle her. The only thing that caused was her eyes to flutter.

"Answer me when I'm talkin' to you, bitch! You think you some kind of gangbanger or somethin'? Is that who you are?"

Simone finally spoke up. My li'l sister was one bad and brave bitch. "Nigga, if you gon' shoot me, do it. Stop playin' games and talkin' shit, and pull the goddamn trigger."

He snickered and so did the fat motherfucker who still had a grip on me. His dick was eye level, and I seriously thought about punching his ass, just to get him to release me. But Simone had my attention. I was proud of my sister. She proved to Honey that his threats weren't about shit.

Probably upset by her reaction, he pulled her up from the table and shoved her so hard that she stumbled and fell face first on the sofa. She quickly turned around and eyed him with a devilish stare.

"Bring that other bitch over here," Honey said to his friend. He lifted me by my arm and pulled me over to the desk by Honey.

"I assume that since you're the one with the purse, you got my shit, right?" he said.

I nodded, and when Mr. Fat Ass let me go, I reached into my purse to give Honey his money and credit cards back. I kept my mouth shut, because I didn't want this situation to turn any uglier than it already had. What I didn't expect, though, was for him to count his money. Simone and I had stashed $500 underneath the seat in my car, so in a nutshell, we had come up short.

He snickered again and shook his head. He pulled his wife beater over his head and tossed it on the sofa next to Simone. His chest was buff and every inch of it was covered with tattoos. He then touched the fine hair on his chin and stroked it in thought.

"Sis," he said, looking at Simone, "we have a problem." He turned his wrist to look at the diamond watch that glistened on it. "I'ma give you about two minutes to tell me where my five hundred dollars is. If you don't tell me, all this talk gon' turn into action and your poor mother will have to bury two daughters, instead of one. If you think I'm playin', try me."

I seriously wanted this over and done with. I didn't care if he was all talk, but I was sick of being in his presence. Simone wasn't buying his threats. She tapped her foot on the floor while rolling her eyes. "I don't know where yo' five hundred dollars is, and whatever Karrine gave you is all that we have."

He looked at me, but I came clean. "It's in the car. I'll go get it, just so you can stop with yo' damn threats."

His eyes shifted to the big dude whose only job was to take orders. "Take Simone outside to get my goddamn money. Tear their fuckin' car up to find it if you have to, but don't come back in here empty-handed."

Simone didn't bother to move, but that didn't stop dude from pulling her up and throwing her over his shoulder. She swung out wildly and pounded the hell out of his back with her tightened fist. "Let me down, you ape-ass-lookin' nigga! I'm not gettin' shit!"

"If she's not willin' to get my money, throw that bitch in the basement until she chills the fuck out. Whatever you do, get my money out of the car and bring it to me."

Big man left with Simone thrown over his shoulder. She kept hitting him, but I could tell that the punches hadn't hurt him in no way.

After they walked out, Honey swiped the gun from his desk and put it into one of the drawers. He then went over to the double wooden doors and locked them. He turned to me and eased his hand in his pockets. We stared at each other and his light brown eyes stayed connected with mine until he came within inches of my face. I inhaled his cologne then sucked in a deep breath. Him being this close to me made me nervous, but then again, I was used to it.

"Did you have to be so mean to her?" I asked. "And BJ almost broke my damn arm for real. I guess that fat motherfucka havin' a bad day."

Honey touched the side of my face and rubbed it. "Sorry about that. But you know I had to handle that li'l situation like any nigga would."

He pecked my lips, and a few seconds later things got heated. He turned me around and bent me over his desk. With my legs spread, he reached around to the front of my pants and unzipped them. He then pulled them over my curvy hips and yanked them down to my ankles. As I stepped out of my pants, he massaged my ass and had my whole body blazing with fire. His touch was so smooth that my legs started to tremble. I could barely keep my balance in high heels.

"This is such a beautiful sight," he said, standing behind me. "Next time, don't stay away from me for so long."

"No, next time, don't let yo' dick stay hard when my/your sister is fuckin' you. I saw how hard you were with Simone. Did you forget that she was really your sister?"

"Don't make me explain that shit right now, ma. We'll get into that later. Right now, I got about ten minutes before BJ come knockin' on that door. You know damn well he ain't gon' be able to hold Simone down for long, so why waste time on why my dick stayed hard for her? You should only be worried about how hard it is right now for you."

"Yeah, nigga, whatever. Spin that shit how you wish. You lucky my pussy cravin' yo' ass right now."

Honey eased his hand over my mouth to shush me, and as he put on a condom, I waited patiently for him to slide his hard muscle into me. After he moved his hand from my mouth, he held my hips and eased my pussy on his dick like it was a warm, fitted glove. My ass jiggled as I backed it up to him, and with each pounding thrust, it jiggled even more.

I was so damn crazy about Honey. We had been on this fuck fest for over a year now. Yes, he was Ray's son, but breaking fucking news . . . I wasn't Ray's daughter. I found out that tad bit of information several years ago, when I met Honey at a club. Ray was there too, and I questioned why the two of them looked so much alike. I also questioned why I didn't look like my sisters, and I begged Ray to tell me the truth. He told me who my real father was. Said that he had been killed about ten years ago in downtown Chicago.

I never asked Mama why she hadn't told me the truth, and to this very day, she wanted me to believe that Ray was my father. I hated her for lying to me about that shit, and it was no secret that Mama cared more for Chyna and Simone more than she cared for me.

It was always me and her who couldn't get along. That was because she could tell I suspected something. My eyes showed that I wasn't satisfied with her ongoing lie, but her look always said that she dared me to question her about it.

Just like when I questioned her about Ray being killed. She wasn't down with my questions. She didn't want to talk about it, and when I forced her to, that was when all hell broke loose.

Thing was, I wasn't all that mad at Mama. But I was mad enough where I had started to plot against her. We all had our secrets and this was one of mine. Honey told me about Mama contacting him to set up Simone. He told me where they would be, and I knew how all of this was going to unfold. There was no hard feelings whatsoever for my sisters, but they were just caught in the middle of a little beef between Mama and me. She thought Honey was on her side, but, realistically, he was on my side. I stopped him from killing Mama, because I didn't want her dead. Just hurt for what she had done or maybe crippled to the point where she could no longer be around to get up in our business. A nursing home, maybe, where we could only go see her if/when we wanted to. Something needed to be done, because I was to the point where I wanted her away from me and out of my life. More than anything, she needed to know her place. I couldn't let her get away with taking the only man I had ever loved away from me.

Honey knew she was responsible for Ray's death, too. He wanted to kill her. He knew that Chyna was the trigger-happy bitch who killed Ray, but Honey backed off on his plans when I told him what Ray had done to Chyna. He understood why she wanted her molester dead, but like me, he didn't understand why Mama continued to hold grudges revolving around the past, and she had done many of the conniving things that she'd done.

Her actions had his life fucked up and mine too. He reaped the benefits of Ray's drug money, but when Ray was killed, Honey also lost a lot of hookups. Some niggas wanted to do business with Ray and Ray only, so Honey suffered some major setbacks. He wasn't pleased about that shit, and I wasn't pleased about never knowing who my real father was. I always felt like the black sheep of the family, and Mama had no problem making me feel that way.

Honey ground his hips hard to stir my pussy juices. I loved the way he pushed every inch of him into me and my pussy was one happy bitch. He definitely put a smile on my coochie lips, and as I neared an orgasm my legs got weaker. Honey picked me up and straddled my legs on his muscular, strong thighs. All I could do was hold on to the desk and hope that I wouldn't fall and bust my head when I got mine.

"I need you to pound that shit haaaarder!" I spoke through gritted teeth. "Haarder, baby, fuuuck me haaarder!"

Honey picked up the pace and damn near turned my ass red he pounded it so hard. We both were out of breath, and right after I came, he lowered my legs. He hurried to sit me on the desk, and with my legs spread, he dropped his face between them. His tongue licked my pussy like it was a sticky lollipop. My fists were tightened and my toes were curled against my shoes. Just that fast I was about to cum again. And when he tickled my pearl with the tip of his curled tongue, I squirted his lips with more of my juices.

"Stoooop," I whined and tried to push him away.

He loved for me to serve him my pussy, and he was an expert at eating it, too. I figured he had been fucking with several other bitches, but none of that was any of my business. This was strictly a fuck thing between us. There wasn't a chance in hell that I would get caught up with an addictive dick like his. Too many motherfuckers wanted it. The way I looked at it was there was enough of this good shit to go around. I wanted the next bitch to feel like I did, especially when she got her orgasm. I couldn't blame her for crying out for more. She could count on Honey to give it to her. He was that kind of nigga when it came to fucking, and "satisfaction guaranteed" was his middle name.

The reason he liked me so much was because I didn't ride his dick all the time. When I saw him at the clubs, I didn't confront him over no silly shit about being with other hoes. He didn't have to wine and dine me unless he wanted to and his money didn't mean shit to me. Now, he'd given me some from time to time, but I never asked for it. He said it was just because. That was good enough for me.

He was still trying to mop up my juices with his tongue, but I had had enough. I didn't want

Simone to get suspicious, so I used my heel to push Honey away from me. He stumbled backward, looking sexy as shit. His jeans were still gathered around his ankles and he cupped his big dick in his hand.

"So, that's how you gon' do me, huh? You gon' get yours, but not let me get mine?" he said with a crooked smile that displayed his sexy dimples.

"Lookin' at the condom, you did get yours. And if you want to get some more, it'll have to wait until next time. Pencil me in after I come back from Vegas. I'll be thinkin' about you while I'm there and you better be good while I'm away."

Before I hopped down from the desk, Honey took off the condom and moved forward. He laid his dick between the creases of my pussy and playfully beat it. His package was hard enough to go back in, but ain't no way this motherfucker was entering my hole without a condom. He knew it and I knew it too. But that didn't mean I wouldn't let him tease me.

Honey's dick simmered down, and while still standing in front of me, he held huge chunks of my ass cheeks in his hands. He showed his pearly whites and licked across his thick, sexy lips that I loved to suck on.

"Fuck pencilin' me in. Yo' ass better have that pussy on lock while you're in Vegas. I don't want you bringin' me no leftover shit, and if you do bring it to me, I'ma put a major hurtin' on that sweet shit you got for sure."

"Don't tempt me, because I know how good it feels when you hurt me. Now, please get your clothes back on so I can get the hell out of here. I don't know how the fuck I'm goin' to explain this shit to Simone."

"No need to. I'll explain it for you."

We both hurried back into our clothes. Honey unlocked the door then lit a tiny candle to clear the sex smell in the room. He told me to go sit on the sofa and he sat in the chair behind his desk. He had capitalized on Ray's drug selling business as much as he could, and he still had plenty of connections that ran from city to city, state to state, and country to country. He was doing it up big. But after so many years of doing this shit, all he was known as was Mr. Collector. His circle of real friends was small, and so many people respected his hustle. If he had any enemies, I didn't know about them. I was sure he did, though, because he was one of those niggas who kept his ears and eyes wide open.

Honey winked at me from across the room then hit the intercom button. "BJ, bring that bitch back in here."

A few minutes later, BJ came through the door with Simone in front of him. He dropped a stack of paper on Honey's desk, smiling as if he had just won the lottery. Simone still had a mean mug on her face. She wiped snot from her nose then rubbed her wrist as if it hurt. I rushed up from the sofa and reached out to hug her.

"Are you okay?" I asked. She didn't say a word, but she hugged me back.

"After you went outside to get my money, did you have fun in the basement with my pets?" Honey asked. "I hope my snakes didn't bite you, and I'm pleased that BJ took you on a little tour around the place for acting nasty toward me."

"Fuck you," Simone hissed then backed away from our embrace. "Let's go, Karrine. And, bastard, you'd better hope that I never see you again."

I added my two cents, too. "Take those snakes and slither them up yo' ass. You got what you wanted so stay the fuck away from me and my sisters. Family don't operate like you do, and we don't want no part of you."

Honey placed his hands behind his head and nodded. "BJ, show these bitches the door. It's a disappointment that family can't get along, but Ray always told me that you can't trust hoes in high heels, even if they're your sisters. Maybe

I'll see y'all at the family reunion; then again, maybe I won't."

BJ escorted us out. That sneaky white bitch, Trice, was watching us near the T-staircase. She worked as Honey's snitch. It was how he knew what was going on in the streets. She used to be one of his best customers, but he so-called cleaned her up and gave her a new start. He told me that he trusted her more than he trusted some of his boys, but that made no sense to me. Just like anybody, she could turn her back on him with the snap of her finger, just as I would one day do Mama.

Chapter Thirteen

Chyna

It took Simone and Karrine like forever to get back from Honey's crib. I had started to get worried. I paced the floor in the kitchen, but stopped when I saw Mama standing in the doorway. A silk scarf was tied around her head, and she used Kleenex to wipe her running nose.

"What's got you so uptight?" she asked.

"Nothin'. Just thinkin' about somethin' that happened yesterday."

Mama opened the fridge and removed a container of orange juice. She poured some in a glass then asked if I wanted some.

"No, but thank you." I was short with Mama because I didn't appreciate how she handled herself yesterday. It wasn't like she hadn't put her hands on us before, but it was how she went about that shit that made me feel the way I did. "Are you sick?" I asked.

"Yeah. I'm coming down with the flu and it got me on my ass. I'm also upset because I lost a substantial amount of change at the casino. I don't feel like doing anything, and I'm trying to get well before we go to Vegas. When I go there, I know I'll be able to get some of my money back."

"You mean, you hope you'll be able to. You take risks with gambling and you never know if you'll leave with a frown or a smile on your face."

Mama remained silent, but from the look of her tired eyes, I could tell her plate was heavy, and that she had more than the flu and losing money at the casino on her mind. I was looking forward to our Vegas trip. We all needed to get away. Besides, going there always meant money; there was a lot of it to be made there.

After Mama finished her orange juice, she put her glass in the sink. She started to leave the kitchen, but I called out to her.

"Is everything good with you?" I asked. "You've been actin' kind of strange lately. I also wanted to get at you about those rules you laid on us the other day. You pretty much know that ain't gon' work, Mama. All stuff like that gon' do is have us at each other's throats. You know that, don't you?"

"We're already at each other's throats. Open your eyes, Chyna, and stop walking around like a blind woman who can't see shit. I'm going back into my room to get some rest. Please don't interrupt me. I don't give a care what you and your sisters do tonight. We'll discuss those rules sooner rather than later, so don't think I've forgotten about them."

She walked off, but I didn't understand what she was trying to say. Was she implying that we were at war with each other? I wasn't feeling that at all. All I witnessed were a few disagreements among all of us that could always be worked out.

"Mama, you didn't answer me," I said loud enough for her to hear. She was almost near the steps and on her way upstairs. "I asked if you were all right, because this new attitude of yours ain't cool. If I've said or done somethin' to you, I want you to tell me. There is no doubt that we fucked up with Honey, but all I can do is apologize for that. I'm sorry. It was a big mistake that won't happen again."

Mama sneezed then wiped her nose again. She came up to me and cracked a tiny smile that seemed forced. "That's what you said the last time, Chyna. You said it was a mistake when y'all stabbed that bitch in the back in St. Louis and left her for dead. You said it was a mistake when y'all cut up that trick down the street tires because she looked at y'all the wrong way, and you said it was a mistake when I had to do two years in prison because my damn daughters shot at an innocent teacher who y'all thought had dissed a friend that neither of you bitches talk to anymore. I took the fall for that shit, remember, Chyna? This shit is getting real tired and old. You just can't keep on making mistakes. We have a good life, and we don't need to be doing no gangbanging shit that can send us to jail. I said it before and I'll say it again: use what you got and use it to the best of your ability. The only power you need to use to get by is the power of your pussy. Using it in the right way will take you far places in life. Using it in the wrong way will send you six feet under. The choice will always be y'all's to make, so think like a wise one. Now, I'm going to bed. Simone and Karrine should be back soon, so stop pacing the goddamn floors and wearing them out. Honey called and said their slick mouths could have gotten them hurt, but as their brother, he didn't feel up to the task. If he did, just think about all the trouble we could find ourselves in right now."

Mama left me in the kitchen in deep thought. She had been riding that nigga Honey's nuts, and I didn't like it one bit. It was no secret that we had done some excessive shit that didn't make sense. Maybe it was time for me to sit down and have a for real talk with my sisters. They both looked up to me, and if I had the capabilities of shutting some of this mess down, then I would try my best to do it. Mama was starting to seem real stressed by our actions. That was the last thing I wanted.

Karrine and Simone rushed inside almost fifteen minutes later. They laughed about how things went down at Honey's crib and gave me details about it all. I was so glad that I hadn't gone with them. I wasn't sure if I would've been able to handle his disrespect. Pulling on the weave was a no-no, and throwing somebody in the basement with pythons wasn't where it was at. Simone said they were secured behind a glass, but so damn what? That shit was foul.

"Here's the deal," I said to my sisters as they leaned against the kitchen counter. "Mama is sick and she needs a break from us tonight. All I have is three appointments set up, along with Mr. Preston. If y'all don't have a lot goin' on to-night, let's get the hell up out of here. I wouldn't mind goin' out to the club, but y'all need to tell me what's up."

"I don't mind either," Simone said. "And to hell with Preston tonight. I don't feel up to it. Tell that motherfucka I'm sick."

"I'm not gon' turn down no paper," Karrine said. "So count me in. I have two hookups on my schedule tonight, but I'll make it quick."

I talked to Karrine and Simone about how Mama was feeling. Since I sometimes called the shots, I told them to chill for a while on bringing the unnecessary drama around. It was starting to fuck with Mama's head.

With that being said, we left that night, knowing that there was no room for error. But as soon as we got to the club, some unexpected shit popped off that was beyond our control.

It revolved around Simone and that nigga Reno. He was on her like flies on shit in the club, and when she tried to walk away from him, he yanked on her arm and wouldn't let go.

"Come here, bitch," he said. "Don't walk the fuck away from me, especially when I'm talkin' to you."

I was on the crowded dance floor and saw everything unfold. Simone pulled away from him, but he continued to be aggressive. Her face scrunched and she grabbed his dick in her hand, squeezing it. Reno's mouth formed in a wide circle and saliva started to drip from it. He was in a whole lot of pain. I could tell by the way his eyes rolled to the back of his head that his dick was suffering.

"Nigga, back the fuck up and take yo' li'l-dick ass somewhere and chill before I crack these nuts and make them bleed," Simone shouted. "I've been called too many bitches in one day and my limit has been reached! All of this disrespect is totally uncalled for, and you should have left that noise you bringin' at the door."

Simone released Reno's dick, and right in the middle of the floor he dropped to his knees. The colorful lights kept on spinning, the DJ kept kicking down music, but the crowd on the dance floor had spaced out. One of Reno's boys came on the dance floor to help him. I figured that once he got his balls in order, Simone was going to catch some major heat.

Dressed in tight-ass jeans that hung low on my perfect waistline, I walked toward the table where Simone and Karrine sat. My braids hung down my back and a pink flower that matched the pink and yellow half shirt I wore was clipped in my hair. With the shirt being cut right underneath my breasts, my abs were on display, as well as my silky chocolate skin.

Niggas were turning their heads, whispering and trying to pull me in every direction. I paid them no mind. I was trying to find out what had happened between Reno and Simone. Four other dudes were at the table with them, and everybody was tossing back plenty of alcohol. My mood had gone downhill after seeing the incident with Simone and Reno, but she appeared to be upbeat.

"Girl, sit down and stop being so overprotective," Karrine said to me. "Have a drink and don't let Reno spoil the fun. He shouldn't have put his hands on Simone. That's what the fuck he gets."

"No, Reno shouldn't be runnin' around here lyin' about fuckin' a bitch when he ain't been in no part of me. I did that shit because his ass been yakkin' and lyin' on me. Ain't no way I'ma let a short-dick nigga like that up in this pussy. Please."

Simone rolled her eyes and they all laughed, including the dudes who were sitting at the table spending hella money on drinks, hoping that it would buy them a piece of ass tonight. Little did they know, it wasn't going to buy them shit but conversation and a few fake laughs.

One of the dudes scooted over in the booth. "Sit next to me wit yo' sexy-ass self. Stop lookin' so mean and enjoy yourself. If that fool come over here trippin', me and my boys got yo' back. Meanwhile, let me buy you a drink. Then, I wanna get to know you better."

His conversation was weak as fuck. I ignored him and sat at the booth on high alert all night. Karrine and Simone had been up dancing and flirting with every nigga who walked by our table. I followed the direction of Simone's eyes when she stared straight ahead then shook Karrine's shoulder. The person we saw coming our way was Honey. He was with several of his friends. Just when I thought the night couldn't get any worse, it did.

Honey rocked a crisp white button-down shirt and baggy jeans. His locs were in a ponytail, and the shine on his chocolate skin was nothing to play with. A diamond cross hung from his neck and money breezed through the air as he walked. I had to admit that my long-lost brother was one fine-ass nigga. His hooded eyes were glued to Karrine the whole time. Hers were locked on him. At first, I couldn't tell if I saw fear in her eyes or lust. Then, it hit me. I'd seen that look before. Her gaze showed some kind of attraction to him. She didn't turn to look away until he approached the table with two beat-face niggas next to him.

"Well, well," Honey said with a smirk on his face. "My li'l sistas up in here stealin' all the thunder. Y'all makin' noise and spreadin' mega love to the niggas who ain't deserving. I thought that after what had happened today, y'all would be somewhere in hidin'."

Karrine ignored Honey while sucking her teeth to keep quiet. Simone folded her arms and didn't dare hold back on him.

"Well, well, well, sorry, but you thought wrong, brother. Ain't no need for us to be in hidin', so just keep it movin' and pretend that you didn't see or hear us up in here makin' noise."

Since I'd missed the happenings from earlier, I had to let this fool know that we wouldn't be bullied by him or by the thugs he brought to the table with him. "Honey, it's good seein' you again, and better with your clothes on than off this time. Let's stop the childish games and learn how to forgive and forget. You got yo' shit back, so please tell me why you felt a need to come over here and say somethin' to us. From my understandin', you didn't want to see our faces again. I promise you that we ain't excited about seein' yours either."

He massaged the hair on his chin while nodding his head. "I see you got a lot of mouth too, Chyna, but all a big bro wanted to do was stop for a second to say what's up to my trouble-makin'-ass sistas. Since I'm not welcome in y'all's presence, let me step so y'all can keep on givin' these niggas up in here heart attacks. I'm surprised y'all ain't seen no familiar faces up in here from that video porn shit y'all do, but please do be careful because ya just never know who is really watchin' when y'all think they ain't."

He shrugged and strutted away. I'd be lying my ass off if I said he didn't just piss me off. What he didn't know was that we didn't accept gutter, broke-ass, club-going, thirsty niggas in our circle. A motherfucker had to prove that he had some serious paper before we accepted his membership. A few broke fools had slipped through the cracks before, but they were always weeded out when they couldn't fork out the money. Since money had to be paid in advance, the show didn't go on until money was paid in full.

"I need to go to the restroom," Karrine rushed to say. "It's hot as hell in here, and I'm starting to sweat in this tight-ass dress."

Two of the dudes moved out of the booth so Karrine could go to the restroom. I kept my eyes on her until she disappeared in the restroom. Minutes later, I saw Honey walk over by the restroom and stand by the door. When he looked my way, I pretended to be in a heavy conversation with the hot-breath nigga next to me and I laughed.

Simone was being fake too, but she seemed to show interest in a light-skinned dude next to her with low waves. He was kind of cute, but cute didn't always cut it. I wondered if he would be the one to end her so-called virgin status. She really needed to quit with that mess. It was obvious that Reno had gotten a piece of it, and I didn't understand why Simone thought we were foolish enough to believe her. Ain't no way in hell he would've clowned on Simone like he'd done tonight if he hadn't tapped into the pussy.

I narrowed my eyes and peeped through the crowd of partygoers who stood in front of us. Fake smoke clouded the air and my vision was slightly blurred from the heavy weed smoking going on that was burning my eyes. I could still see though, and as soon as Karrine came out of the bathroom, Honey snatched her arm. He pulled her to the other side of the wall where I couldn't see a thing.

Not knowing what the fuck was up, I rushed up from my seat and told Simone that I would be back. I wasn't sure what to expect, but if that motherfucker Honey was still trying to bring drama our way, I was about to let his ass have it. I held a bottle of Moët in one hand and swooped up another empty bottle from a table that was close by the bar. When I felt this one nigga touch my ass, I snapped my head to the side to check him.

"Have some motherfuckin' respect, fool. Did I ask yo' ass to touch me?"

"No, but that big ass you got was so invitin'. I couldn't help myself."

Wrong time, wrong place. I had to keep it moving, but any other time it wasn't going down like that.

I moved in closer to Honey and Karrine and could see him standing closely in front of her. Basically, there was little to no breathing room in between them. They both had smiles on their faces as he rubbed his finger down the middle of her breasts. She moved his hand, but he put it on her hip and squeezed. He then eased his arm around her waist and pulled her closer to him.

In no way could I hear what they were saying, but I damn sure could see what was up. He leaned in to kiss her, and seeing them together damn near broke my heart into a thousand and one pieces when I saw my sister's lips touch his.

Why in the fuck was she tonguing the shit out of her own damn brother? Didn't she hear Mama tell us who the fuck he was? What was up with them and wasn't he the same fool in the motel room that Karrine had taken a shot at? I was confused. First Mama was playing games

with this nigga Honey, now Karrine. Was he our
brother for real? He sure did look like Ray, but
none of this made sense to me.

The only reason I didn't have time to stay there
and figure it out or question them was because
I saw Reno and his friend rushing toward the
table where Simone was. She was all by herself,
meaning without me or Karrine. I suspected that
none of those thirsty niggas at the table had her
back like they said they would.

In a hurry, I bumped into a bitch who was
dancing next to several of her friends and
wouldn't move.

"Excuse you, tramp," she hissed. "You didn't
have to bump me like that."

"Well, move yo' non-dancin' self out of the way
or take yo' stiff ass to the dance floor then."

She and her friends called me all kinds of
names, but I saved my issues with them hoes for
another day. I continued to rush toward the table
with both bottles tightened in my hands and
lowered by my side. By the time I reached the
table, Reno was up in Simone's face, talking shit.
He squeezed her cheeks with his hands and she
was trying to get a grip on his neck. As expected,
the other dudes had scattered. The one who
was with Reno smiled at the action. With the
dude's back facing me, I snuck up from behind

and smashed the Moët bottle against the back of his head. I saw a wide gash appear and blood started to ooze from it. He staggered backward and slumped on a table before falling to the floor. He grabbed the back of his bloody head, and tried to call out to Reno, but he'd already seen me. I met his gaze with a slap across his face with the other glass bottle. It shattered and the whole left side of Reno's face split open. Blood sprayed my clothes and some got on Simone. More people around us started to break out running, as if someone had yelled fire.

"Fuckin' bitch," Reno yelled and tried to come after me. He didn't get far, because Simone jumped up from the table and kicked him right between his legs. For the second time tonight, he dropped to his knees. This time, however, he needed serious medical attention. We quickly fled the club along with everyone else. It wasn't until we were outside when we were able to catch up with Karrine.

"Hoochie mama, where were you?" Simone yelled at her. "Did it take you that long to use the toilet? I thought you got hurt. Shoot!"

"Naw, I'm good. I saw Ki-Ki from the beauty shop. I stayed in there hollerin' at her for a while. I hadn't a clue what was going on, until I saw everyone running."

Lying bitch. I didn't say one word about what I'd seen. The truth behind all of this would come to the light. Whenever that happened, I expected much hell to break loose.

Chapter Fourteen

Taffy

I despised bitches who always thought they could outsmart me, especially the ones who I'd given birth to. It was my blood that ran through their veins, and every single thing that they learned, they had learned it from the head bitch in charge. There wasn't a game that they could play that I hadn't already played. There wasn't a nigga they could fuck or suck who I didn't already know about. The fact that they believed I wasn't paying attention irritated the fuck out of me, and slight cold or not, I was always on top of mine.

Like always, whenever I walked into the room where they were, it fell silent. Eyes shifted around. Their heads turned in the other direction. That was always a signal that somebody had something to hide, and since they'd gone clubbing the other night, I suspected there was trouble.

I didn't bother to ask questions, only because I had some other shit that needed my immediate attention. I had to nip this shit in the bud before it got seriously out of hand. It involved Karrine. This bitch was about to be the death of me if I didn't hurry to get her in check.

Dressed in my all-white pantsuit, I was ready to go handle some business with Honey. Most of my braids were in a tight bun on my head, but a few braids dangled along the sides of my face. My jewelry was always sparkling, and whoever that bitch Ashley Stewart was, she damn sure knew how to hook up a sister with curves.

I put the strap to my silver Coach purse on my shoulder and looked directly at Karrine. The girls were watching a reality TV show in the family room. With it almost being 7:00 p.m., I figured they'd be getting ready for their gigs soon.

"Get up, Karrine, get your jacket and go with me. No need to change into anything else. Your pajamas will do just fine."

She stood up and looked down at herself. "I can't go nowhere like this. Give me a minute to put on some clothes."

See, this was starting to be too much for me. Nobody didn't listen to shit I said. It was like they wasn't even trying to hear me. "Let me repeat myself. No need to change into anything else. Your pajamas will do just fine."

She stood with her lips pursed, displaying too much attitude. "Okay, but where are we goin'? I hope not too far."

"Far enough. Now do like I told you to. I don't have much time."

Karrine sighed and left the room. She was lucky that I didn't punch her in her face. I was steaming inside and the frown on my face showed every bit of my anger. Chyna and Simone questioned me about where we were going. I wouldn't say.

"Don't worry about it. When that bullshit y'all watching come off, be sure to clean up the kitchen. Those clothes in the laundry room need washing; and who left the empty carton of ice cream in the freezer?"

Simone pointed to Chyna and Chyna pointed to her. They both laughed, but as mad as I was, I didn't see shit funny. "Somebody go get it and throw it away. It don't make sense to leave it in there; and don't forget to take out the trash, too."

They got into a serious argument about who left the empty ice cream container in the fridge. I was in disbelief as I stood in the kitchen with a banging headache while drinking a Diet Coke. I didn't know what was taking Karrine's ass so long. *If she comes back in here with clothes on, God help us.*

As Chyna and Simone argued about who was going to remove the empty ice cream container and take out the trash, I slammed my Coke can on the counter. I walked over to the freezer and snatched the container out of it. I hurled it across the room, and unfortunately for me, it could only hit one of them. Chyna just happened to be the one.

"Tag, bitch, you're it," I shouted. "Pick up the goddamn container and take the fucking trash outside. You motherfuckas are starting to work my nerves! Must everything around here turn into a battle? Damn!"

Chyna picked up the empty container and threw it in the trash. She took the trash outside. That was all she had to do in the first place.

If that incident weren't enough to work my nerves, when I heard heels clacking on the hardwood floors, I swung around. Karrine's ass was dressed like she was going to prom. I guessed she'd figured that since I was dressed up, she needed to be dressed up too. That shit didn't work for me. She saw me charging her way and started running to get away from me. I couldn't believe that I had to chase that heifer up the stairs, but when I caught her by the ankle, you best believe that she was tumbling down fast. Her ass bumped down each step. I yanked on her leg and pulled her toward me. I could barely catch my breath. Dirt from the bottom of her shoe got on my white pantsuit, leaving me pissed. So pissed that I twisted the fuck out of her ankle.

"Oooo, okay, Mama," she whined. "Let it go, please. I'm sorry. I just didn't want to go nowhere lookin' tacky."

"Tacky or not, get yo' ass upstairs, change back into your pajamas and put on those damn bunny slippers you always wearing around here. Meet me in the car in ten minutes or else I will pack up every piece of your shit and make you my first homeless child."

I let go of Karrine's ankle. Even though she pouted, she limped back up the stairs and did what she was told. I refused to go any-damn-where with this dirt stain on my white pantsuit, so I went into my closet and put on a red pantsuit, brought to you by my girl, Ashley Stewart.

I returned to the kitchen and saw Chyna and Simone doing what they were told about washing the clothes. Saying nothing else, I waited in the car for Karrine. Almost nine minutes later, she came outside with her head hanging low. Her light pink pajamas were suitable for the occasion and so were her bunny slippers.

Karrine got in the car. The first thing she did was open her mouth again. "Would you please tell me where we're goin'? That's the least you can do, since you got me out here lookin' like a damn fool."

"And the least you can do is shut the fuck up until we get to our destination. If you got questions for me then, at that time, I'll be happy to answer them for you."

We rode in silence. Lord knows I wasn't trying to be mean to my girls; no, that wasn't me. They were just out of control. I had no one else to blame for the spoiled, ungrateful bitches I'd created. They all needed to grow the hell up, and maybe it was time for me to set them free. I wondered if they'd be able to make it without me. One of these days they would have to do it. All the lies and secrets were starting to get underneath my skin, but starting with Karrine, today she'd have to come clean and answer for her fuckups.

Karrine's eyes grew wide when she saw me park in Honey's driveway. She didn't even want to get out of the car. When she did, she moved like a turtle as she walked to the front door. I rang the doorbell. It didn't take long for Trice to open it. A smile was on her face and she reached out to give me a hug.

"Hello, Taffy," she said. "It's so good to see you, and as usual you're always lookin' spectacular."

I pulled away from Trice and smiled. "You know I wish I could say the same for you, but I can't. Girl, you need to leave that alcohol alone because I can smell that shit seeping through your pores."

Trice laughed and so did I. It's how we got down with each other. I'd known her for years. I was the one who had gone to Honey and asked if he would help clean her up. She was more of a loyal friend to me than she was to anyone.

Karrine trailed behind us with an attitude, and when the double wooden doors to Honey's office came open, he was sitting behind the desk with the phone pushed up to his ear. He held up one finger, gesturing that he would be done in a minute.

"Get that swoll look off your face and sit down," I said to Karrine. "I'm getting tired of looking at that ugly face. I just knew that when you saw Honey you'd have something to smile about."

All Karrine did was fold her arms. She continued to sit back on the sofa with an attitude. She pretended not to be fazed by this, but I figured her mind was going a mile a minute. After all, I wasn't supposed to know about her shenanigans. I bet she was wondering how in the world did I ever find out.

Honey's fine black ass sat behind the desk looking just like Ray. He actually looked better than Ray. I loved it when his locs were pulled away from his face and into a ponytail. I understood how Karrine could find herself caught up with him, but what I didn't understand was why she thought it was okay to betray me? Her own goddamn mother who had done everything, everything that I could for my girls.

Honey ended the call and stood up. He walked around the desk and stepped forward to hug me. "What's up, Mama," he said. "I apologize for takin' so long, but I needed to handle that."

"No problem, sweetheart. But you do know we have a problem with something else."

He nodded and walked over to Karrine. He leaned down to kiss her cheek, but she held up her hand. "Please back the fuck away from me before you get smacked. I don't know what the fuck you and Taffy are up to, but please tell me why I'm here."

I cocked my head back and chuckled. "So, I'm Taffy now, huh? 'Mama' when yo' ass needs something, but 'Taffy' when I ain't shit. You know damn well why you're here, Karrine. Maybe you should tell me why you think you are."

Honey leaned against his desk and folded his arms. I went over to a bar in the far corner and poured a glass of Hennessy.

"Mama, I could have gotten that for you," Honey said. "But—"

I quickly cut him off. "But my ass, Honey. You could have gotten it, but you know how y'all ungrateful asses are."

I swirled the glass around and looked at the brown liquid before tossing it to the back of my throat. It burned, but I poured another glass then took a seat in the chair behind Honey's desk. No one said a word until I lit a cigarette and whistled smoke into the air.

"Karrine, I'm waiting to hear your side of this story, unless you can't talk because you still got Honey's dick shoved down your throat. Or you may be thinking about all that good dick he gave you, but it don't look like you will be getting any of it today."

She winced and rolled her eyes. "Fuck Honey. I couldn't care less about his ratchet dick. I'm more concerned about why you never told me that Ray wasn't my damn father. That me, Chyna, and Simone were only half sisters. All this other stuff don't even matter. You were the one who kept this secret for years, not realizing that I needed to know who my damn daddy was."

"If you wanted to know, bitch, all you had to do was ask. Don't sit there and try to pretend that this was all about not knowing who your daddy was because it's not. It's about you wanting to be in control, Karrine. I assure you that that's something you will never have. It's all about you trying to be bigger than me. There is only one bitch who will run this show and that's me. Now, if you think you are big and bad enough to bring me down, go for it. I brought you here today to give you options, options that can keep you in my circle or that can lead you right out that door and into a world of the unknown. You decide, because at this point, what you decide don't matter to me one bit."

Karrine sat silent for a minute. She looked at Honey, who was staring at her. "Why you keep lookin' at me, traitor?" she hissed.

"I'm lookin' at your bunny shoes and laughin' my ass off because I've never seen you dressed like this. And I didn't mean to put you in no situation like this, ma, but you was gettin' ahead of yourself. You needed to pull back on that noise you was talkin' about Mama. I've never been upset with her about a damn thing, only because

I knew, firsthand, what kind of animal Ray was. I saw him put his hands on her for no reason. I also knew what he'd done to Chyna. Ray and I were close, no doubt, but I wasn't down with a lot of shit he did. As for me and you, Mama felt like she couldn't trust you. She was right. She felt like she couldn't trust Simone. She was right about her too. Y'all wonder why she always on Chyna's team, but Chyna the only one who be down with her no matter what. Y'all gotta learn how to fall in line too, 'cause this lady right here would lay her life down and die for all of us, ma. We need to start showin' her a little mo' respect. You feel me?"

I wasn't sure about laying my life down for no damn body, but I loved Honey, truly I did. He wasn't my biological son, but he was the closest thing I had to one. He was there to witness all that Ray had done to me. When he beat me and threw me out in the cold, I remembered Honey looking out of the window with tears flowing from his eyes. When Ray kicked me down the stairs and I lost my first child, Honey stood on the stairs and reached out his small hand to help me. Time and time again, he was there. My girls had no idea what Honey meant to me. If any of them ever got serious with a nigga, I'd want him to be just like Honey or better. The only problem was he and I were too close and his ass would never be faithful to Karrine. I doubted that any man could be faithful, but that was just me. Regardless, I feared that his involvement with Karrine would do more harm than good. With that in mind, this shit had to cease.

Shame covered Karrine's face. It had been a long time since I'd seen tears well in her eyes. I didn't raise no weak women, so I got up from my chair and stood in front of her. I lifted her chin and could tell that she was fighting back her tears.

"Keep those tears locked away. There ain't no need for them. Let this shit be a lesson and whatever you do, don't let it happen again. I'ma chalk this shit up this time. Next time, Karrine, you have my word that I won't do it. This shit is between you and me. Chyna and Simone don't need to know nothing about today. They don't need to know what's been going on between you and Honey. You can keep on fucking him if you wish, but I'm here to tell you that you need to make sure that nigga is strapped up tight, because he eats, breathes, and sleeps pussy all day long. He is capable of breaking your heart, and if he does, I'll have to kill him. You don't want me to do that, so give his ass a nice, juicy, wet kiss tonight and make your exit while you can."

Karrine looked over at Honey. He had the widest smile on his face. He knew he was a ho, so therefore, he couldn't be offended by anything I'd said.

"I'm so sorry. I should have known better," Karrine said to me.

She stood and reached out to embrace me. I held her tightly in my arms. The shit felt good. I loved all three of my daughters, and even though I had my favorite, it wasn't by much. Karrine not having the same father as Simone and Chyna didn't cause me to love her any less. It was she who had this thing with me. I was glad that we were putting all of this bullshit behind us.

I let Karrine go and looked into her big, round eyes. "Your father was gay. Ray had done me so bad that I started fucking with somebody else. I was vulnerable when I met yo' father, and I was desperate to be with anybody other than Ray. I ignored the signs, and when I went to his apartment one day, I saw him getting fucked in the ass by another man. I was already pregnant with you, but I went back to Ray and told him that you were his child. When you were born, he found out that you weren't his. I paid dearly for lying to him. I begged him to never tell you the truth because I was embarrassed to have a child by a gay man. I never wanted you to know him, and when he died from AIDS, I thought that ended it. My hope is that today it does end, and that we never have to talk about this shit again."

Karrine released a deep sigh and sat back on the sofa. She kept expressing how sorry she was, but I'd already forgiven her. Sometimes, my kids got the hell out of line, but it was my duty to put their asses back in check. I saw this as a celebration moment, so I told Honey to pour all of us a glass of Henny so we could toast. We stood in a circle and lifted our glasses in the air.

"Here's to the future. With our heads on straight, may we all make millions and not kill each other before we reach billions."

Karrine and Honey laughed. Afterward, she gave him a kiss, but it was too long for me. I pulled her away from him. "You know I don't play that shit. All I said was kiss him good-bye, not get his dick hard so you can come back and suck it later. Go to the car and cool yo' hot ass off. I'll be there in a minute."

Karrine thought I was playing, but I wasn't. I told her again to wait for me in the car. After she left, I stayed to have a quick chat with Honey.

"I need some money for our Vegas trip," I said to him. "We're leaving next week and you know it's going down, don't you?"

"I'm sure it is," he said, opening his drawer and pulling out a checkbook. "Be safe and bring Karrine back to me in good condition."

"Nigga, you'd better leave her alone. Just so you know, I'm dead serious about hurting you if you hurt her. Do you think I'm playing?"

"No, I know you're not. But we got this bond thing goin' on that's kind of tight. I'll just say this: if she don't pursue me, I'll back off."

"And I'll say this: find another piece of pussy to tear into because your playtime with Karrine is over. Don't fuck this up over no pussy, Honey. I know you're much better than that. Also, I don't take checks from nobody. Deposit the money into my account. It needs to be there within the next thirty minutes because I got some extra shit that I need to take care of before I go."

Honey closed the checkbook and rubbed his chin. "Anything else, Mama?" he said sarcastically. "Please tell me if I can do anything else for you before you go."

Yeah, his tone was shitty, but every now and then I had to wake him the fuck up too. I was the bitch in charge of the whole empire he was running. With the snap of my finger, I could have him removed from the throne and shut this shit down. Only Honey and I knew how involved I was in the business. The only reason I didn't let the girls know was because I wanted them to learn how to make a living for themselves and not rely on my money.

I picked up the glass with Henny in it and tossed it in Honey's face. He squeezed his eyes then jumped up from his chair. He wiped his hand down his face, but before he could speak up, I brought him back to reality.

"One: check your tone because I don't play that sarcastic bullshit." I slapped the shit out of Honey, causing his head to jerk to the side. "Two: that was for punching Simone in her stomach. Nigga, don't you ever do that again. We will always play by my rules, not yours. Now, give Mama a hug so I can go." I held out my arms, but he just stood there staring at me.

"Just so you know," he said. "One day you gon' push me over the edge. When that day comes, I do feel sorry for you."

"Yeah, that's what all my kids say. And just so you know, when Taffy Renee Douglas goes up, she ain't coming down. So never feel sorry for me. The only people you need to feel sorry for are your sisters and yourself for being blessed with a wonderful mama like me."

Honey let out a cackling laugh as he walked me to the door. That bastard never did give me my hug, but fifteen minutes later, I checked my account and the money was all there. I knew he was good for something other than sticking his dick where it didn't belong.

A little over a week later, we were ready to jet to Vegas. Bags were packed and me and my lovely girls rushed to the front door to leave. Our Louis Vuitton luggage was filled to capacity with clothes, shoes, and accessories, but it looked like Vegas would be on hold, especially when I saw two police cars pull in our driveway. My heart raced, and I dropped my luggage on the floor. The girls stood behind me with their arms folded and attitudes washed across their faces. I wondered what in the fuck had they gotten themselves into now. This shit was ridiculous. I heard Simone whisper, "Reno," to her sisters, and my foot was on the verge of swinging into somebody's ass.

Chapter Fifteen

Taffy

We had waited for weeks to get the fuck out of Chicago and have some for real fun in Vegas. My gut told me that there would be a quick change in plans, especially when one of the officers stepped forward.

"How can I help you?" I asked the familiar- looking officer who had come to our townhouse before.

"Taffy," one of the officers said, "we need to speak to your daughters about an incident that happened at a club the other night. May we come in?"

I backed away from the door. So did Chyna, Simone, and Karrine. The one thing I had taught them about the police was to be respectful, answer questions as truthfully as you can, and never let them see you sweat.

By looking at the girls, I could tell they were prepared. We all stood in the foyer, awaiting the officer's questions. I didn't know what the hell had happened, but I was surely tuned in.

"A few witnesses said that Reno and Jarred were injured by some young ladies named Chyna and Simone. The club owner is not happy about the thousands of dollars' worth of damages, and he's looking for reimbursement. Would either of you ladies like to tell me what happened?"

Chyna spoke up first. "What happened was, from a distance, I could see Reno with his hands around my sister's neck, chokin' her. Her eyes were rollin' to the back of her head and it looked like she couldn't breathe. I knew that I couldn't handle Reno and his friend by myself, so I picked up a few bottles from the table and went upside their heads. It was all done in self-defense. If the owner turns over the tapes so you can see them, you'll see that everything I just told you was the truth."

"Which one of you is Simone?"

Simone raised her hand. "Me, I'm Simone."

"Why did Reno, allegedly, have his hands around your neck, choking you?"

"Because he's been tryin' to get at me for quite some time and I wasn't havin' it. He'd been lyin' to people, tellin' them that he had sex with me and that's untrue. I confronted him earlier that night, and he came over to my table later and we got into it. He put his hands on me first. Thank God my sister was there to stop him from killin' me. What we did was in self-defense. Period."

The officer took notes and sighed when Simone continued to tell him what a jerk Reno had been to her. Chyna mentioned an incident on the dance floor and she stressed how Simone was trying her best to stay away from Reno.

"Okay, ladies, here's the deal," the officer said. "I'm going back to the club to look at the tapes. If your stories don't jibe with what I see, I'll be back with an arrest warrant. And you all may want to think about how much money you want to give the club owner for his troubles. His place got severely damaged from people rushing to get out of there. He's considering lawsuits. I'm sure there's a way to resolve this matter without going to court."

I quickly spoke up. "If you don't mind me saying, Officer, I have two problems that I need to discuss with you before you leave. First of all, we're on our way to Vegas. I'm not going to reschedule my trip. Second of all, I don't understand how a bottle upside a nigga's head can cause a club to get damaged. The owner should have insurance if anything happens to his club, and we're not going to offer one dime to him for renovations. You can let him know that I said so. If he has a problem with that, then we will see him in court."

"I'll pass the word on to him, but as for going to Vegas right now, I wouldn't do that if I were you. Like it or not, your daughters are in the middle of an ongoing investigation. If this thing goes to court, it may look like your daughters attempted to flee."

My blood was starting to boil, but I tried to remain calm while the officers were there. They stayed for a while, running police checks on all of us and continuously talking more about the incident at the club. After that, they hit us with those famous fucking words I hated to hear: "We'll be in touch. Soon."

As soon as the officers left, I locked the door and turned to my slick-ass daughters who couldn't keep their asses out of trouble for nothing in the world. I put my hand on my hip and let out a deep breath from being frustrated. "Now that I may have to reschedule our trip to Vegas, which one of you bitches gon' pay me back for it?"

They all looked at each other, but didn't say one damn word.

"Yeah, that's what I thought. By the end of the day, I need five thousand dollars for my goddamn troubles. I'm not going to reschedule my trip, but y'all assess gon' stay right here. Before I go, I need to talk to this muthafucka Reno. I don't believe shit y'all say these days, and if he tells me that y'all started that shit at the club, somebody gon' be packing up their shit and getting the fuck out of here. I just can't keep doing this with y'all. This is the last straw! Now, where does his ass live? Better yet, go get in the fucking car. Take me to this fool so y'all can tell me how this shit went down face to face with that nigga."

"Simone is the only one who knows where he lives," Karrine said. "I don't know, and I'm not goin' anywhere because I didn't have anything to do with it."

"Shut the hell up. You don't have options. When I tell you to do something, just do it! Now, go get your happy-go-lucky ass in the car, or you'll find yourself laid out on the goddamn floor with my foot stuck far up in you."

Karrine ol' smart-mouth ass pouted then stormed out the door. So did Simone. Chyna told me that she had to use the bathroom and would join us in the car in a few minutes.

With thick wrinkles lining my forehead, I followed Simone to her car. Karrine got in the back seat and I got in the front. A few minutes later, Chyna locked the front door and joined us. Simone pulled out of the driveway, and we all sat in silence as she drove down the street.

Trying to calm my nerves, I lit a joint and blew much smoke in the air on purpose. Simone covered her mouth and coughed. She looked over at me.

"You know there ain't no smokin' in my car, right?"

I nodded. "And you know you'd better shut the fuck up talking to me and keep on driving, don't you? Bitch, in case you forgot, I paid for this damn car. I will smoke, fuck, shit, do whatever I want to do in here, whether you like it or not."

Simone pursed her lips while looking straight ahead. She clamped her mouth shut. Chyna, however, scooted close to the front seat and reached for my joint. "Gimmie a hit of that, Mama. Please. I need something to calm my nerves."

I jerked my head to the side then snapped my fingers in the shape of a Z. "No. So sit yo' tail back and stop breathing down my neck. I don't share anything with troublemakers. All you need to be doing back there right now is praying."

Chyna winced and sat back. "Okay then. Lord, please help my mama to stop trippin' and bein' upset over dumb stuff that we ain't have no control over. Hopefully she'll see that we ain't lyin' to her and then she won't have to miss her Vegas trip. Thank you. Amen."

Chyna stared out the window after delivering her so-called prayer. I guessed she thought this shit was funny. We'd all soon see who would have the last laugh. I looked at Simone as she slammed on the brakes to avoid hitting a white man on a bike.

"Daang," she shouted out the window. "Move out the way, fool!"

He shouted, "Fuck you," to her and she lost it.

"Fuck you too, you slimy, ugly bastard!"

"Girl, go run that slick-talkin' muthafucka over," Chyna said. "Run his ass over, check his pockets, and keep it movin'."

Simone was about to do it. I grabbed the steering wheel, turning it in another direction. Simone slammed on the brakes again, but the car still hit the curb.

"Are you bitches crazy?" I shouted. "Y'all must be on some medication that my ass don't know about. I can't believe you about to do some dumb shit like that."

"I sure was," Simone said. "His ass don't know me to talk no shit like that. I was gon' run him clean over and rock-a-bye that bitch."

I put my joint out then reached over to put Simone's car in park. Maybe we needed to have a little talk about some things, because my daughters were clueless as fuck.

"Larry, Curly, and Moe, listen up. If y'all think there are no consequences for running over a white man on a bike, in broad daylight, then y'all are bigger fools than I thought. The police will hunt you down and make sure you get ten life sentences for doing some bullshit like that to a white man, so learn to think before you act. If that muthafucka was black, the result may not be the same. Either way, stop doing stupid shit that can turn yo' life around in an instant. I'm not gon' always be here to rescue y'all from this bullshit, so get a clue and act like I taught y'all better than this. I'm in this car because I want you to take me to this nigga Reno. I'm not here to do anything else, and if you want to play the knockout game with bikers, do it on your time, not mine."

Nobody said a word, not even Karrine's big-mouth self who always had something smart to say. Simone drove off and I cranked up the volume on the radio, listening to Trinidad James. I then looked at my watch, wondering if I could still make it to the airport. "How much longer do we have before we get to Reno's place?"

"About ten minutes. He don't stay too far from here."

"Tell me a few things about this fool, just so I know who the fuck I'm dealing with."

Simone shrugged her shoulders. "All I know is he's a drug dealer, he got a lot of hoes, and he's a punk."

"That's all you know about a man who you let get the cookies?"

She got real defensive and started rolling her neck around. "Excuse me, but I've never had sex with Reno. He's been lyin' to people, tellin' them that we got up, but it ain't true."

"Well, Reno ain't the only one who is lying. So are you, and if the dick wasn't good, it just wasn't good. Ain't no need for you to disown it, after you done gave it up."

Chyna and Karrine laughed. "I know, right?" Karrine said. "Simone know she done fucked that man, so stop lyin' about it."

Simone kept with her lie. "If I had given him the goodies, I would say so. I didn't, so get over it."

"Look," I said, "get your panties out of a bunch and stop with the attitude. I'm the only one entitled to have one right now, so chill. I will say this, though. Ain't no man gon' be acting a fool like y'all said he was at the club if he ain't sniffed, ate, sucked, or dipped into the pussy. Niggas don't get down like that, so you can keep lyin' all you want to, Simone. The only person you're playin' is yourself."

"Tuh, I know that's right," Karrine said.

"Whatever," Simone replied then rolled her eyes. She had nothing else to say and neither did I.

We pulled into a parking spot at Reno's apartment complex a little after noon. A few kids were outside playing on a playground that had four swings, but three of them were broken. Trash was piled high in Dumpsters and the areas where there was supposed to be grass there was mud instead. I surely didn't want to sink my red bottom shoes into no mud, so I was careful to stay on the concrete path that led straight to Reno's door.

"Is this where that nigga brought you to, to have sex?" Karrine asked Simone. "I know damn well you can do better than this."

Simone didn't bother to reply. I was wondering the same thing myself. This nigga was a cheap-ass drug dealer to be living like this. Simone needed her ass kicked for fucking with a fool who didn't even know how to spend his money. She knocked on the door and we waited for an answer.

"Who is it?" a man yelled.

"It's me. Simone. I need to talk to you."

Reno opened the door then cocked his head back when he saw all of us standing outside. He wasn't a bad-looking nigga. Kind of reminded me of the rapper Drake, but with darker skin. At least she had good taste in men. That was all I could give her credit for.

"What's this? A family reunion?" he said with sarcasm in his voice.

"If that's what you want to call it," Simone said, "fine. Can we come in?"

Reno opened the door. The first thing we saw was a skinny bitch on the couch, eating some barbecue-flavored potato chips. I knew a crackhead when I saw one. She damn sure fit the bill.

"Bitch, you gon' need to make a move," Reno said, pointing to the door. "Holla at me later, all right?"

Whoever the woman was, instead of checking his ass for calling her a bitch, she looked us over and pursed her lips. She then reached for her purse on the coffee table with cigarette burns on it.

The apartment had a funky, dirty sock smell to it. There wasn't no telling what else I smelled. Whatever it was, it assaulted my nose and made it sting. And the more I looked around, the more I concluded that this nigga was trifling. The whole apartment was fucked up, roaches climbed the walls, dishes were piled high in the sink, and the hand-me-down furniture hadn't enhanced the apartment one bit.

After the woman left, Reno locked the door. I could see the white bandage on the back of his head. Had a vision of what Simone and Chyna had done to him. Without a shirt on, he stood by the door with his hands in his pockets.

"So, what brings all you fine, troublemakin' bitches in my hood today?"

Strike one. The girls folded their arms, but I stepped forward. "Let me make myself clear, before we get off on the wrong foot. There ain't no bitches in this apartment right now, unless yo' mama is back there in one of those nasty-ass rooms, waiting to school yo' ass on how to be a real man and clean up after yo' fucking self. I came here to find out what happened at the club the other night. If my daughters were in the wrong, I want to know about it."

"Hell, yeah, they were wrong, but two wrongs will make it right. They will be dealt with. That ain't no threat; it's a promise."

Strike two.

"As for the bitch thing, Miss Mama, I call it as I see fit."

I turned to my girls who had a "we told you so" look on their faces. I wanted to give this nigga the benefit of the doubt, but I wasn't going to waste another minute with him. Besides, I had to catch my flight to Vegas. I figured I'd be delayed at the airport or would have to take another flight.

I held out my hand and snapped my finger. "Strike three. Chyna, give it here," I ordered.

Chyna reached behind her and pulled out the Glock 9 that she'd gotten while we were at the house. I knew my daughters well. She must have known that it would come in handy when she said she had to use the bathroom while we were back at the house. She tossed the gun to me, and catching everyone but her off guard, I turned the gun sideways and pulled the trigger three times, causing me to jerk backward. The bullets whistled in the air, before landing right into the center of Reno's chest, busting it wide open. Blood splattered as his back slammed against the white door and his eyes bugged in shock. His trembling, bloody fingers wiggled in front of his chest, and we all watched as he slid down the door then fell on his ass. His head slumped then his body tilted over and hit the floor.

Chyna smiled, Simone covered her mouth, and Karrine appeared to be frozen in time. Somebody had to pay for the delay of my trip. This smart-mouth motherfucking nigga seemed like the perfect choice.

"Take a deep breath," I said to my daughters. "Straighten your backs and find me five thousand dollars for my troubles before y'all get out of here." I reached in my purse and distributed black leather gloves to each of them. "Don't touch a damn thing. I'll be waiting in the car. Y'all got five minutes before I pull off, and I will pull off because Vegas is awaiting me."

I put my gloves on and kicked that lousy motherfucker away from the door with my red bottom shoes. I hated to use my shoes on this trashy nigga, but I wasn't about to touch his ass, gloves or no gloves.

When I opened the door, the crackhead bitch was sitting on the steps. She looked at me and I looked at her. "You didn't see me and I didn't see you, right?" I said.

"No, ma'am, I didn't see a thing."

"Good." I reached in my purse then pulled out a hundred dollar bill and gave it to her. "Make sure you keep it that way or else I'll be back."

She nodded and watched as I headed to the car. I used my cell phone to quickly call Honey.

"What up," he said.

"Got 'im. This petty nigga been stealin' from us for a long time. No more worries on this end. It's a wrap."

"Sounds good," he said. "Enjoy Vegas, and I'll see you when you get back."

I ended the call and my thoughts turned to Reno who had been a thorn in my side for a long time. He had a bad reputation in the streets, and he'd been cheating Honey out of his money for a long time. Honey hired him to handle his business over four years ago, but Reno had been smoking up the product and he always made excuses about being robbed or the police being after him. Anybody who fucked Honey, fucked me. While Reno had never seen me a day in his life, it was unfortunate that we had to meet like this today. My girls didn't know shit, and this little incident was about more than me having their backs. They would definitely see it that way, and I damn sure was going to let them keep on thinking it.

Less than five minutes later, they came running out of Reno's apartment with several things in their hands. They hopped into the car and the tires screeched as I drove off.

"Let's see what we got here," Simone said, opening a black bag with jewelry inside.

I could certainly see the platinum, gold, and diamonds from where I was sitting, so I knew she was on to something. Karrine had a wallet that had several hundred-dollar bills inside, and Chyna had three black socks that were stuffed with cash too. She scooted forward and waved the bills near my face.

"After givin' you yo' five Gs, do I get to keep the rest?" she asked.

"No," I said, snatching the money from her hand. "Drop all of that shit on the floor up here, 'cause we ain't divvying up shit. I'm getting the hell out of here for a while. Y'all can stay at home and wait until that officer returns. Deal with it, ladies. Handle yo' business, because Mama is going bye-bye."

I went back to the house to get my luggage, and almost six hours later, I was happily on my way to Vegas with plenty of money in my pockets to spend.

Chapter Sixteen

Chyna

I didn't give a damn what anybody said about my mama; she was all right with me. I loved that woman to death and I was glad that she was on vacation, doing what she loved to do best: gamble.

That left me, Karrine, and Simone at the crib doing our thing. I was gearing up for a long night in front of the computer monitor and was looking forward to it, too. Video porn relaxed me, and after what had happened today, I was a little worried that the police would come to the house and arrest us for Reno's murder. I was glad that Mama had put that nigga out of his misery because he deserved it. And like she said, think before you act and speak. You just never know who the fuck can say the wrong shit to, and Reno's ass had finally met his match.

If or whenever the police came back to the house, the plan was for us to keep our mouths shut. We didn't know anything, and everybody who knew Reno, they knew he'd had hella enemies. I suspected that fingers would point to me and Simone, but finger-pointing didn't mean shit. The only person who kind of knew how that shit went down was that crackhead chick who was at Reno's apartment. I was going to make some calls later, just to be sure that she wasn't running her mouth. If she wasn't, she was good. If she was, then I'd have to deal with her myself. Mama had done her part and the rest was on us.

Another thing I intended to deal with was this situation with Honey and Karrine. Ever since what I had witnessed that day at the club, they'd been on my mind. I had to be careful about my approach because Karrine was known for saying the wrong motherfucking thing sometimes and setting me off. She needed to come clean about that situation. It was time that I knew the truth.

Before I went to work tonight, I knocked on her bedroom door then opened it. Karrine was lying across the bed while talking on her cell phone. The moment she saw me, she ended the call.

"Who was that?" I asked. "Honey?"

She frowned as if I didn't know what was up. "Why would I be talkin' to Honey?"

I walked farther into the room and sat on her bed. "Because, Karrine, I saw you kissin' him at the club. What's up with that? Ain't he supposed to be like our brother? I don't get what's goin' on with you lately. I'm startin' to feel like you ain't down with us no more."

Karrine started to bite her nails. "I'm always down with y'all, Chyna, you know this. It's just that me and Mama have our issues sometimes 'cause she be trippin'. As for me and Honey, I guess it really ain't no surprise to you that Ray really wasn't my daddy. So, technically, Honey is you and Simone's brother, not mine. I met him years ago and we hooked up. By then, I knew the deal with Ray, and Honey and me been seein' each other ever since."

"I'm not surprised about Ray either, but this thing with Honey is a shock to me. So, in other words, when we went to the motel to rob him that day, you knew who he was? And not only that, but he was fuckin' Simone. That's nasty. I don't understand how you're down with that shit."

"Simone was the one who got on top of him. If she had known he was her brother, she wouldn't have gone there. But ain't nobody tell her that she had to fuck him. That was on her and it has nothin' to do with me."

"I disagree, but you're you and I'm me. I don't like the idea of you fuckin' with Honey. Somethin' about that whole thing leaves a bad taste in my mouth."

Karrine just shrugged her shoulders. "I can understand how you feel, but what do you want me to do about it? And just in case you don't already know, I'm not fuckin' with him no more. Mama put closure to that bullshit. She don't want us to see each other anymore."

"I know what me and Mama want, but what do you want? Are you in love with him or what? Are you goin' to continue to see him, even though we're against it?"

"I'm not in love with nobody. Don't know love, don't show love, unless it's for Mama or for the love of my sisters, right? That's how it goes, and for now, I'm stickin' to it. I may have my gripes about shit, more than you and Simone do, but that's just me."

I stood and reached out my arms to give Karrine a hug. I understood how she felt. My only hope was that she meant what she'd said about her love for us. Lately, I hadn't been feeling it.

"I need to get out of here so I don't be late for my ten o'clock appointment. How many dates do you have tonight?" I asked.

"Six or seven. I need to get dressed too, so I'll holla at you in the a.m. I'ma take me a long nap afterward; then we'll hit up breakfast at IHOP, okay?"

"Maybe so. I'll let you know for sure."

I left Karrine's room, feeling good about her being honest with me, but still skeptical overall. We had been keeping so many secrets from each other, like the one I'd been keeping about my man on the side. The thing was, I really liked Marc too. He was the kind of nigga who I could see myself one day marrying and having a whole lot of babies with.

With me being the oldest sister, I really wanted to start a family. I still had dreams of moving away with my family, but me and my man would always live close by. Marc and I had been kicking it for about two years, but not on a regular basis. He lived in St. Louis. I had to drive there to see him, or he had to come here to see me. He had a decent job in the real estate business and his paper was long. We talked on the phone at least four or five times a week, but sadly, Marc had no idea what I had been doing in the privacy of my bedroom. I told him that I worked in sales. Whenever he'd come to Chicago, I invited him to a one-bedroom apartment that I'd gotten over a year ago. That was where we'd met. Nobody knew that I'd had the apartment, nor did they know where it was. I had to keep it that way, because I was certain that Mama wouldn't approve. Maybe not even understand that, even though I was happy, at least by the age of thirty I wanted to be out of this house for good, living in Cali or Miami and being with the man of my dreams.

While thinking about Marc, I changed into a royal blue baby doll negligee made of sheer material. It accentuated the color of my chocolate skin perfectly. With my long braids falling way past my shoulders, I looked like a million bucks. Before my first appointment, I picked up my cell phone to call Marc.

"What's up, li'l mama?" he said, putting a smile on my face.

"Nothin' much. Just gettin' ready to go hang out with my sisters. I wanted to call and tell you that I'll be there tomorrow around noon. Do you want me to meet you at your loft or at your office?"

"Meet me at my loft. The key will be underneath the mat so make yourself at home. I have a short meeting at twelve thirty, but I should be home after that."

"Okay, boo. I'll see you tomorrow. Until then, be good."

"You too, ma. Luv ya."

"Me too."

We ended the call. I was so hyped about seeing Marc tomorrow that I put on one hell of a show for my clients. I'd already had about three orgasms, just from imagining that the dildo I was riding while on the bed was Marc's big dick sliding in and out of me.

"Give it to me, daddy," I shouted while riding the dilly and spreading my ass cheeks so that Gregg could see it easing in and out of me while looking at his monitor. I let out a painful groan each time the dilly went into my dripping wet pussy.

"Gregg, I don't know what I'm goin' to do with you and this big dick! No other man has ever fucked me like this. You sure do know how to make a bitch's pussy dance for you."

I released my healthy chocolate ass cheeks then backed it up closely to the monitor.

"Lick me, daddy. Stick yo' tongue in my pretty pussy and lick me all over. I want to feel your tongue deep in there, baby. Get it far up in there."

I couldn't see if Gregg was licking the screen, but his words told me that he was.

"It's so pretty, Dynasty. I could eat this shit forever. I love to watch my dick and tongue turns circles in you. Get on your back so I can see all of it. I want to taste all of you."

My play name was Dynasty, and this time, I faced the monitor and spread my legs wide. I scooted my pussy as close to the screen as I could get it and toyed with my pearl as Gregg "licked" me.

"Cum for me, baby," he said. "Squirt that shit at me, so I can see how good I've been to you."

Within a few minutes, I faked an orgasm that satisfied Gregg. His time was up, so I blew him a kiss then waved good-bye.

After cleaning myself up and changing into another negligee, I was on to the next nigga for the night. I didn't get finished with my gig until almost four in the morning. When I went to Simone's room, she was asleep. Karrine had just wrapped up a session and she was down for the count too.

"I'm goin' to sleep," I said to her as I stuck my head in the doorway. "I may have to miss breakfast in the mornin'. Since Mama is in Vegas, I'm gon' take advantage of it and get away for a few days. You think you and Simone will be okay?"

"I hope so. Tell your mystery man I said hello. If Mama calls, what do you want me to say?"

"Say what you always do. You don't know where I'm at and I'm not in yo' back pocket. Tell her to call me. I'll answer my cell phone."

"Will do. Get some sleep 'cause you look tired. So am I. I sholl hate we missed out on goin' to Vegas. Wherever you're goin', don't go too far, just in case the police come back to question us."

"I won't. I'll be in the area. You can call me, too, if they do show up."

Karrine said that she would call me. She picked up her phone to make a call then got in the bed. I closed her door, but instead of going to sleep, I packed up a few things and headed to St. Louis.

It only took about four hours to get there, and if anything happened at home, it wouldn't be hard to get back. I needed to get the fuck away for a few days. I hadn't seen Marc for about two months. I hated our long-distance relationship, but for now, it worked for both of us. I was always hyped to see him. This time was no exception.

Marc lived in a downtown loft that required a code to get in. Once I put in the four-digit code, I took the elevator up to the ninth floor. I knocked on the door first, but when I got no answer, I looked underneath the mat for a key. It was there, so I unlocked the door and went inside.

Marc's loft only had one bedroom, but it was laid the fuck out. It was a huge open space with hardwood floors, a double-sided fireplace, a balcony that viewed the Gateway Arch, and a kitchen that any chef would adore.

I tiptoed to his master bedroom, but he wasn't there. The king bed was covered with black silk sheets and fury, fluffy pillows. Black art covered the walls and scented incense burning gave the room a cinnamon smell. Marc must've just left, because I could still see the dripping wet shower inside of his spacious bathroom. I reached for my cell phone to call him.

"Yo," he said in a playful manner.

"I'm here. I just got to your loft and you got it smellin' pretty damn good in here."

"I did that just for you, because my funky socks tend to take over when I know you're not coming. Make yourself at home and don't be eating up all those chocolate-covered strawberries in the fridge that I bought for you. Save me some."

I walked to the fridge. Inside were some chocolate-covered strawberries and a dozen red roses. Marc could tell by my silence that I was looking at them.

"Those are for you too," he said. "I hope you like them."

I smiled and shared a little love with my man. "I do, and thanks, babe. I love you."

"Not as much as I do, but I gotta go. I'll see you in a bit, all right?"

I told Marc that I would see him soon and made myself at home. Knowing that all we would do was fuck the day away and chill, I changed into a silk, button-down pajama shirt that cut right above my knees. Marc had some chicken breasts in the fridge, so I decided to make me a grilled chicken salad with ranch dressing. As I started to prepare the food, my cell phone rang. It was Karrine calling.

"What up?" I said.

"Where are you?"

"Away."

"Away as in far away or close by?"

"Close by," I lied.

"Well, the police are here to talk to you and Simone. They're downstairs, but I told them that you went to the grocery store and would be back soon. Can you make it here or not?"

"Unfortunately, I can't, but handle that shit, Karrine. Y'all need to stop dependin' on me for every doggone thing and learn to take care of shit if I'm not there."

"The problem is you said that you would be here if I called, and the last time I checked you and Simone were the ones who did that shit to Reno at the club. What if the police are here to talk about what happened at his crib? What the fuck am I supposed to say?"

I released a deep sigh. "Get a clue, Karrine. Say what the hell you wish, or better yet, just keep your mouth shut and don't say nothin'. Is that so hard to do? I won't be home until Sunday. Until then, do you."

Karrine hung up on me, and even though I told her to call me if anything went down, I had hoped that, for once, they could have my back and handle shit while I was away. I was seriously to the point where I was getting tired of seeing about everyone else. What about me? I had a life too, and being with Marc made me feel as if I had a bright future ahead of me. I couldn't help but to think about us, but then my thoughts turned back to my conversation with Karrine. I felt bad about the shit. I hated to go off on her, but when I called back to apologize, she didn't answer. That had me worried. What if I needed to be there to speak to the police myself? I called again, and again, and after the fourth time, Karrine finally answered.

"What?" she said in a nasty tone.

"Listen. I apologize for—"

"No need. I'm busy and I'll see you whenever you get home. Bye."

She hung up the phone. I was upset, but I figured we would deal with the situation when I got back. For now, I pushed the drama with my sister to the back of my mind and decided to do something special for my man.

After making my salad, I went to Marc's bedroom and sat on the bed. I ate my food, and since I hadn't had any sleep, I lay across the bed and shut my eyes. It felt like I had been asleep for several hours, and when I woke up, I felt soft pecks on my legs. I looked at Marc dressed in a white crisp shirt, black slacks, and a multicolored tie. His suit jacket was thrown on the bed and his watch was next to it. The waves in his hair were flowing tough and his face was shaved clean with a little hair left on his chin. His skin was as chocolate as mine and smooth.

"Wake up, sleepyhead," he said. "How long have you been asleep?"

I stretched my arms then sat up on the bed. "Too long, I guess. What time is it?"

"Almost four o'clock. Sorry I'm late, but my meeting ran longer than expected."

"It's okay. I needed the rest anyway."

Marc stood up and started to remove his clothes. I watched his sexy, near perfect body that was muscular and covered with a few tattoos on his chest. Years ago, Marc was a boxer who was on his way up. Everything went downhill after that, when he went to prison for selling drugs. When he got out, he decided to change his life around and do the right thing. I appreciated that. If anything, I needed a man who could be an inspiration for me.

Marc lay on top of me. I opened my legs wide, inviting him in. I still had on my pajama shirt, but there was nothing underneath it. We shared an intense kiss, before he started to take bite marks down my neck.

"You smell delicious," he said. "Mmmm. I can't wait to taste you."

I was pretty damn eager for him to get busy too. It had been a minute since I'd had sex with anyone. Throughout my life, I'd only had three sex partners. I was always reluctant to give the goodies to just anybody.

Marc started to unbutton my pajama shirt. My breasts escaped from it and he started to suck them. He massaged them in a circular motion, lightly pressing them together. I was on fire as his tongue turned circles on my nipples and my pussy was already tingling. I was sure that Marc could feel the beat of it, thumping against his hard dick that was on the verge of pushing into me.

But he didn't go there just yet. He pressed his thick lips down to my belly button and stopped to suck it. I giggled because it tickled then I pushed his head down to go lower. He did, but before diving in, he stretched my pussy lips apart to expose my cherry drop that peeked at him through my slit. He hung his tongue over it and allowed a few drips of his saliva to cool it down and wet it.

It appeared wet enough for him, so he dove right in. His curled tongue and fingers were in action at the same time, causing me to tighten my fists and curl my toes from the intense feeling that was breaking me down, minute by minute.

"You know you my nigga, don't you?" I said. "Get that shit, baby, do that shit real good. I promise I'm gon' take care of you like you allllways take care of me!"

Marc took care of me so well that I quickly squirted his face with my juices. He didn't even let me go down on him, and before I could do anything, he put his overly thick dick inside of me. Marc was so thick that he filled my pussy to capacity. I could stretch no farther and every inch of my slippery walls were touched by his heavy meat.

"You feel wet, warm, and sticky, Chyna," he said while on his knees and watching his dick glide in and out of me.

I was on my elbows watching it too. His dick entering me was a pretty sight. The look of it was even better than the feel of it. I eventually had to close my eyes, so I wouldn't cum so quickly again.

Marc had had enough of watching his performance. He poured my chocolate legs over his shoulders then pushed my legs close to my chest. His hips turned in slow, rhythmic, deep circles, and when he sped up the pace, I knew it was time to let the fucking begin. His body slapped against mine, so hard that you could hear the smacking sound echo in the room. I threw that shit back to him and we seemed to be in a battle over who could fuck who the best.

As horny as I was, I was starting to win. Marc couldn't keep up with my fast pace. He fell back on the bed, looking defeated. I straddled him and wore his ass out. Rode him tough, only like his Chyna doll could do. I moved over to the edge of the bed and used the floor for leverage as I rocked the squeaking bed. The headboard slammed into the wall. My body began to drip with sweat and so did his. My pussy started to hurt, but I kept on going. His hands were squeezed into my hips, trying to slow me down, but I wasn't having it.

"Fuck me, ma," he shouted. "Girl, fuck this dick like you own this muthafucka! Show daddy how much more I can get out of this pussy. You haven't given it all to me yet, have you?"

Like hell I hadn't, but I was surely about to give him more. I picked up the pace and made my pussy throb like a heartbeat, squeezing it tight then releasing it. Each time, Marc's body jerked. I could feel his dick thumping too, and minutes later, he sucked in his bottom lip and bit it. He lifted the upper part of his body from the bed and his grip on my hips got tighter.

"Yoooou, you got me, ma. That pussy got me! Daaaamn!"

No question, it did. A flood of his juices swam inside of me. In an effort to get mine, I crawled up to his face and let him go to work again. It didn't take long for me to cover his lips with heavy cream. After that, we were spent. I lay next to him in bed. Both of our chests heaved in and out.

"Why . . . why you wear my ass out like that?" Marc said while softly rubbing his chest. "Yo' ass is bad, Chyna. You were horny as fuck!"

"Yes, I was. And I'm still horny. We need to make up for some of this lost time, don't we?"

"You ain't said nothing but a word and we will continue. Right now, though, I got something that I want to give you."

Marc got out of bed and went into his closet. I had the pleasure of seeing his nice ass that I loved to grip and his limp dick that was still meaty, even if he wasn't hard. I turned on my stomach and laid my head on my crossed arms.

I wondered what Marc had gotten for me now. He'd had a habit of always buying me nice things. This time, whatever it was, was behind his back. I watched as he walked over and kneeled down in front of me. He moved several of my long braids away from my eyes and placed the strands behind my ears so I could see.

"I need you," Marc confessed. "And every day that you're away from me, I'm miserable and I feel lost. We've been together long enough for me to recognize some things. And that is, Miss Chyna Douglas, that I want you to become Mrs. Chyna Wilson real soon. Set the date; tell me when I need to be there and I will."

My breathing had already halted. My eyes were bugged, and I kept blinking away the tears. I couldn't believe that Marc had asked me to marry him until he brought forth a black suede box from behind him and flipped it open. I was blinded by the sparkling diamond that had to be the most beautiful piece of jewelry I'd ever seen.

"You ain't saying nothing, so I'm a little worried," Marc said.

I still hadn't said anything because the first thing that came to mind was Mama and my sisters. Yes, I wanted this so badly and there was no doubt about it that I loved Marc. But was this the right timing? Was this the man I wanted to spend the rest of my life with? I knew that he was, but I kept telling myself that he wasn't. Why? Because I figured that no one would approve of this. Not one single person, but this wasn't about them anymore. It was about me being happy. I deserved it. I couldn't let this opportunity pass me by.

I leaped off the bed and threw my arms around Marc's neck. I playfully kissed his cheeks then his lips, shouting, "Yes! Hell, yes, I will marry you! I love you, man, damn I love you!"

"I love you too." He laughed. "But yo' ass is heavy. You ain't pregnant, are you?"

"Not yet, but by the time I leave here, maybe I will be."

I surely didn't lie about that. We had fucked our way into early Sunday morning. I was supposed to leave sometime this afternoon, but I found it so hard to depart from him. I kept gazing at the ring on my finger and thinking about planning our wedding. I wanted to share the good news with everybody, but I had to tell Mama first.

When I picked up my cell phone and turned it back on, I had several missed messages. Three of them were from Karrine, telling me that it was urgent and I needed to call home. Two calls were from Mama, and when I called her, she picked up right away.

"I'm just returnin' your call," I said. "How's Vegas?"

She hesitated to speak up, but finally did. "Where are you?"

"I'm at a friend's house."

"Who?"

"Marc's house. He lives in St. Louis."

"And why are you in St. Louis when I told you to stay with your sisters, just in case the police came back to the house?"

"Because I'm grown and grown people make decisions to do what they want to do. I don't want to argue with you about this, Mama, and as a matter of fact, I was callin' to share some good news with you. Marc and me been seein' each other for a while. He asked me to marry him. I said yes, and I'm real excited about becomin' his wife."

"Yes!" Mama shouted. "Girl, I just hit the jackpot on this machine! I'll call you back!"

She ended the call. I wasn't sure if she'd heard me. I was a little bothered, but, no matter what, Mama would have to get with the program because this marriage was definitely going down.

Marc left about seven o'clock that morning and said that he'd be back around three. A client of his came from out of town to see one of his properties and he was anxious to sell it to him. He was also hopeful that they would be able to close on the deal today. He asked me to stay around so we could have a late dinner to celebrate before I left. I was thinking about leaving tomorrow, but for now, that was just a thought.

While sitting on the couch with my legs tucked underneath me, I called Karrine, but got no answer. I called Simone too. She didn't answer either. When I called the home phone, it went straight to voice mail. There were times when no one would answer their phones, but with Karrine saying that things were urgent, I kept calling her back.

After my fourth call, a man answered her phone. "May I speak to Karrine?"

"Who is this?" he asked.

"No, the question is who is this?"

"This is Honey. Is this Chyna?"

"Yeah, but what are you doin' with my sister's phone?"

"I don't have her phone, but since you kept calling back I answered it. She's asleep right now. I'll tell her that you called."

"Make sure you do. She said something was urgent, so I need to holla at her soon."

"I'll see if I can wake her. If not, you'll hear from her whenever."

I didn't have time for games, so I ended the call and left it there. Karrine was playing with fire. I wasn't going to interfere with her relationship with Honey, but that was a real dangerous move.

Five minutes later, Karrine called back. "I was trying to call and tell you that Simone got locked up and Mama is home. Why haven't you been answerin' your phone?"

My brows shot up. I couldn't believe what she'd said. "Wha . . . Wait a minute. I just spoke to Mama. She's still in Vegas. Why is Simone in jail? What happened?"

"I told you the police were there. They came to tell y'all that the stories checked out okay. Then they started to question us about Reno's murder, and Simone's mouth got her in trouble. The police officers kept tryin' to pump information from us, and Simone went off on them. She reached out and scratched one of their faces and she got locked up. I couldn't reach you, so I had to call Mama to come deal with the situation. I'm tired of this foolishness, Chyna. I'm sick of Mama yellin' and screamin' at me like this is all my fault."

"She yells and screams at all of us. You just take it more personal than we do. But when I just talked to her, she told me that she'd just won a jackpot while still in Vegas. I don't know why she would lie to me, but oh well. Where is Simone at now?"

"She's at home. Mama got her out of jail, but she probably lied to you because she was upset with you for leavin'."

"She'll get over it. I'll be home later today or early tomorrow. I have some good news to share, but I'm not tellin' you just yet. As for you, what are you doin' with Honey?"

"Nothin'. I just came over here to talk to him. I couldn't reach you, Simone was in jail, and I really needed somebody to talk to. Honey has always been a good listener."

"That's cool. Don't do nothin' that I wouldn't do, and I'll see you soon. Peace, girl, be good."

"You too."

Right after I got off the phone with Karrine, I started to clean up the mess Marc and I had made around his loft. I tidied the kitchen and cleaned the bathroom. Once I was done, I started to watch TV, but faded because nothing was on and I was bored.

Several hours later, I heard a hard knock on the door. I squinted to look at the clock. It was almost two o'clock. I rushed to put on Marc's robe to cover up then made my way to the door.

"Who is it?" I asked.

The person on the other side didn't answer. I looked through the peephole and my heart dropped to my stomach. Mama was at the door, puffing on a cigarette. I was shocked that she knew where Marc lived, but ready to confront her, I released a deep sigh then opened the door.

"Yes," I said, holding the door open.

She dropped the cigarette on the ground then smashed it with her pointed-toe heels. "Congrats on the engagement," she said. "Aren't you going to invite me in?"

I was still in disbelief that she was here. "I am, but I'm a little shocked that you're here. How did you know where I was?"

"Don't ask me any questions. Just be glad that I'm here."

I rolled my eyes then opened the door wider for her to come inside. She was jazzed up in a short jacket, some jeans, and stilettos. Her braids were in a bun, but like always, several tresses dangled along the sides of her round face. Black-framed glasses covered her eyes, but she removed them and looked around at Marc's loft.

"Nice," she said. "Real nice. It looks like your man has done pretty well for himself."

"He has. That's why I'm excited about bein' with him. I hope you'll be excited for me too, but I'on know 'cause you haven't smiled yet."

Mama turned around and reached out her arms. "Come here," she said. I walked up to her and we embraced each other. "I'm always happy when good things happen for my daughters, Chyna. Don't you ever think that I wouldn't be."

"I know you are, but you worry me sometimes. I know how you feel about us and the men we choose to date. That's why I kept Marc a secret."

Mama backed away from our embrace and moved into the living room, where she sat on a circular soft leather black sofa. She laid her leather bag on the table then crossed her legs.

"You may have tried to keep Marc a secret, but when will you ever learn that your mama knows everything? It's important for me to do my homework and I do so very well. Did you think I wasn't paying attention to your trips back and forth to St. Louis? I was, but I figured you would tell me about those trips when you were ready to."

I tightened the belt on Marc's robe then tucked my leg underneath me again, as I sat next to Mama. "I wanted to tell you, but like I said, I didn't think you'd approve. And even though

I know you be watchin' our backs, I wanted you to believe that my St. Louis trips were all about makin' money. They weren't. They were about Marc. We really do love each other, Mama."

Mama smiled then lifted my chin so I could look at her. "I really do believe that you love Marc and good for you. Why don't you tell me about him? If this young man is going to be my son-in-law, I want to know more about him."

I held out my hand and started counting down on my fingers. "First of all, he's very smart and educated. He's in the real estate business, and he makes a gang of money sellin' property and buyin' new property to renovate it, like he did this loft. He's fine as hell; his mother lives in St. Louis and she loves me too. He has two brothers, but he ain't seen his father in years. He used to be a professional boxer, but he did some jail time for sellin' drugs. That was years ago, and he's been on the right track ever since."

Mama nodded her head as I spoke. "He is fine," she said. "Lord knows he's fine, but I'm a little concerned about all of the other wonderful things that you said about him."

My brows rose. "What concerns you?"

Mama reached into her purse and pulled out an envelope. She put her glasses back on, removed a picture from inside, and turned it so I could see it. "Is this the Marc you're referring to?"

I felt the bullshit coming down. All I did was nod.

"Okay," Mama said. "'Cause this right here is Marc Wilson. He dabbles a little in the real estate business, but most of his money comes from drug trafficking. He lives on the south side of St. Louis with his wife and three kids, and they've been together since high school. His mother lives nearby them too, and from what I hear, she loves the hell out of her daughter-in-law and her grandbabies. Both of his brothers are in prison, and Marc will be back there soon, because the police have a close watch on him. His father was killed in 2001, and in addition to all of that, he has a man he's been seeing, too. See, while he was in prison, he had a li'l something going on with another fine nigga he met. Ever since that fool got out of jail last year, the two of them have been secretly hooking up, if you're smart enough to know what I mean. So, if this is the same Marc you see in the picture, please tell me how he is the same Marc you gon' be married to?"

My face had already cracked five times and hit the floor. I blinked away my tears, trying my best not to show hurt, even though I was. I wanted to throw up, and a huge part of me

didn't want to believe Mama. I wanted to call
her a goddamn liar, I wanted to slap the shit
out of her for telling me all of this, and I wanted
to scream at the top of my lungs for being so
fucking stupid. But I knew better. I knew that
I had been calling Marc all morning, but had
gotten no answer. I mean, how many meetings
could one motherfucker have? I questioned why
this place always looked so empty, and as much
as I searched through his things, I never found
anything because there was little searching to
do. Only a few pieces of clothing hung in his
closet, and the linen closet was never filled with
many towels or sheets, only a few. The whole loft
appeared to be just like the apartment that I'd
had in Chicago. It was there for only one reason
and one reason only. To fuck him.

I tried to swallow the huge lump in my throat,
but it wouldn't go down. Instead of forcing it
down, I rushed to the kitchen to get some water.
After I did, I looked at Mama who sat in the
living room, now filing her nails and waiting
calmly for me to respond.

"Do you have the address of where he lives?" I
asked.

"I do, but you have a choice to make. Either
you can pack up your shit and go home with
me, or you can go over there to confront him.

You're going to put yourself in a bad situation if you do, but as always, Chyna, the choice is yours. Not mine."

I left the kitchen and went into Marc's bedroom. I looked at the stained sheets where he'd milked every ounce of cum from me this weekend. I looked at the ring on my finger, and instead of tossing it, I kept it right on my finger. I wanted to throw up and cry like a baby, but a child by Taffy Douglas knew better than to wear her emotions on her sleeve. She had warned us about men. Shame on me for not listening. I put my guard down, even when I knew this relationship didn't feel right. The warning signs were all there. I ignored them because I was desperate to find something better than I'd already had in front of the computer monitor.

Not giving it much more thought, I put on my clothes, packed my bags, and went into the living room with Mama. No sooner than I opened my mouth, though, the door came open and in walked Marc. With confusion on his face, he looked at Mama on the couch then shifted his eyes to the bags I had in my hand.

"This must be your mother," he said, walking into the living room with a forced smile on his face. He extended his hand, but Mama refused to touch it. "Oh, I'm sorry. Did I come at a bad time?"

"No," Mama said. "I think you came at the right time. Chyna, I'll be in the bedroom. Why don't the two of you go ahead and . . . talk." Mama narrowed her eyes and gave Marc an evil stare. She then picked up her purse and went into his bedroom, closing the door behind her.

"I don't think your mother likes me," Marc whispered then laughed.

I folded my arms and sucked my teeth. "Where have you been all day?" I asked.

"I told you I had a meeting. It wrapped up pretty quickly, so we can head out and go to dinner early. I hope you're not leaving this soon. See if your mother wants to go with us so I can get to know her a little better."

"I doubt that that's goin' to happen, Marc, and after a long talk with my mama this mornin', I've changed my mind about us gettin' married. I think it's best that you stay with your wife and kids because they need you way more than I do."

Marc cocked his head back and dropped his mouth open, as if he were in shock. "Wife and kids? Huh?"

"Yes, your wife and kids who you live with on the south side of St. Louis."

The bedroom door came open. Mama poked her head out of it. "You know who she's talking about, nigga. The bitch with the long red hair and light skin. Stop playing games and fess up to yo' bullshit!"

Mama closed the door. Marc stood stunned. He plopped down on the couch, squeezing his forehead as if it ached. "I . . . I was going to tell you about all of that, but the timing wasn't right, Chyna. My wife and I are separated, but I go by there every now and then to check on my kids. I told her that I wanted a divorce and she knows all about you. It's just a matter of time when it will be completely over with us. Then you and I can get married."

My face twisted. I wanted to slap the shit out of him, but I wasn't done with my questions yet. "Really? That's interestin' because how can we get married when you're havin' sex with another nigga, too? Do you think I'm stupid, Marc? Is that what you really think?"

He was starting to get nervous. My mentioning the nigga he was bumping and grinding with wasn't a good thing. The accusation caused him to get angry.

He shot up from his seat like a rocket. "What? I'm not doing a damn thing with no nigga. You are fucking crazy for getting at me about some bullshit like that, ma. I don't know why you're tripping, Chyna. If you just don't want to get married, then say so and stop playing these goddamn games."

He reached for my waist, trying to pull me closer to him. I was so mad that I reached out my hand and slapped the shit out of him. "Back the fuck away from me, you greasy-ass, fake nigga! I'm done with yo' ass and—"

I was caught off guard by Marc's hard blow to my face. He punched me so hard that I dropped to the floor and saw stars. In a daze, I blinked my watery eyes and touched my jaw that felt numb. When I gathered myself a bit, I scrambled to find my purse. Marc shoved me back on the floor and he stood over me, darting his finger at me.

"Yo' ass ain't going nowhere. Tell yo' mama to get the fuck out of here, so that we can deal with this shit right now."

Speaking of Mama, where in the fuck was she? Didn't she know that I needed her right now? This nigga was tripping. Yet again, when I tried to get up, Marc shoved me. This time, he squatted and pulled me by my collar so I could be face to face with him.

"Don't be so damn difficult and do like I tell you to do. Now, get the fuck off my floor and clear that mean ass mug off your face. That ain't no way to look at your future husband. I demand some goddamn respect."

I released a gob of spit in his face. "There's your respect, nigga. Take it and run with it."

While still holding my collar, Marc jerked me back and forth, causing me to hit my head on the floor. When he head-butted me, I screamed out, kicked my legs, and tried my best to fight back. Marc was too strong, though. He punched me in my stomach, and I now knew why he was considered a professional boxer. His blow to my stomach silenced me. So much pain rushed through my body. I could taste blood stirring in my mouth and I was dizzy from being jerked around like a ragdoll.

Feeling as if I was about to faint, I looked over Marc's shoulder and saw a blurred vision of Mama, puffing on a joint. A smirk was on her face and she shook her head.

"Girl, I thought you could do much better than this. I must say that I am disappointed in you."

Marc's head snapped to the side to look at Mama. That was when he stood up and pulled on his suit jacket to straighten it. "Get her the fuck out of here," he said to Mama. "You can get the fuck out of here too. I'm done with trying to turn a ho into a housewife."

Mama took a long hit from the joint then bent over to smash it on Marc's glass table. I knew she was distracting him, just long enough for me to grab my purse off the table and reach for my gun. It trembled in my hand, as I aimed it right at his back.

"Shoot him," Mama said in a calm voice that caused him to swing around and face me. He eyed the gun in my hand and forced a smile on his face.

"Damn, ma, we ain't gotta go out like this. You know I love you, Chyna. Forgive me because I . . . I sometimes get ahead of—"

"Shoot him!" Mama yelled this time.

"Don't," Marc shouted too. "Please don't! I'm so sorry, and if you'll just let me make this up to you, I will."

"Bitch, would you shoot that nigga!"

I didn't know why I hesitated, but I did. My mind kept flashing back to the past few days that we'd spent together and how happy I was being here with Marc. Now, it had come to this. It had come to me pulling the trigger, as he'd made another move toward me. I fired one shot, directly at the center of his forehead. His body collapsed and fell right on top of mine. I pushed him off of me then hurried to scoot away from him. I then rushed off the floor and snatched up my purse and bags.

I was so sure that during the investigation of his murder, my prints would be found all over this place. There was nothing that I could do about that, but if the police ever questioned me, I would stick to my same saying: "I don't know what happened. Wasn't me." The burden of proof was always on the police, but I knew I had better come up with a good alibi in Chicago.

Mama put the strap of her purse on her shoulder. She nudged her head toward the door, telling me to go ahead of her. I did, but when I heard a shot fire off, I damn near jumped out of my skin. Then there was another shot, yet another, and three more after that. When I swung around, Mama stood over Marc and had fired those bullets right into his face.

"Slimy muthafucka," she said with gritted teeth then spat on him.

After that, we left together. She drove back to Chicago in her car; I drove in mine. I was glad about that because I didn't want Mama to see me cry. I was hurt about what had happened. Never would I ever trust another nigga again. I felt like a fool. I knew Mama was disappointed in me. This was the kind of stuff that she'd spent years and years trying to prepare us for. I had failed the test. It wasn't a good feeling.

Hours later, Mama pulled into the driveway. I followed. When she got out of her car, she walked up to me, as I got out of mine.

"It hurt me like hell to hear what that nigga said to you. To see him put his hands on you like that upset me. But I was glad that he kicked yo' ass, just so I wouldn't have to do it. Grown or not, you see now that you can still get your ass kicked, and being grown don't have shit to do with it. The next time you come to me talking about getting married, do your goddamn homework first. Be careful who you love and make sure that muthafucka loves you for real. I'm down with you finding the nigga of yo' dreams, but be smart about the shit. Don't come off as a dumb bitch who ain't been taught nothing. When you do that, you insult me. You disrespect me, and I don't appreciate that shit. Now, get in there and apologize to your sister for chasing dick, instead of being in her corner. Family first, Chyna, remember that shit. Yo' family comes first, because on any given day, we're the only muthafuckas who gon' be there for you."

Mama walked off. I felt horrible for disappointing her. I had to stop telling myself that she didn't have my back, when in actuality she had it more than anybody. I hoped that Simone and Karrine started to realize the same thing too.

Chapter Seventeen

Simone

I could hear Mama and Chyna coming into the house, so I quickly minimized the message that could be seen on my computer screen that gave me chills:

I know who you are, bitch, and I've been watching you! You die! You and your whor-ish ass sisters will die!

My mind started racing a mile a minute. The first person who came to my mind was that crazy fool Blake, who had sent me another e-mail last week asking for me to respond. Since my last response about why I'd robbed him and cleaned out his bank account, I hadn't replied to any of his other messages. I wasn't sure how to handle this situation, and with me just getting out of jail for being a smart-ass, I didn't think this was the right time to bring this to Mama's attention.

Her Vegas trip had been cut way too short. She wasn't happy about it. Then, she had to drive all the way to St. Louis to see what was up with Chyna. She cussed and fussed about that. She and Karrine exchanged a few words, too, so to say the least, Mama was on edge. We had definitely been showing our asses. I had no regrets in speaking to the police officer the way I did. His ass deserved it. There was a way to ask questions, without pointing fingers and making threats. That shit didn't work for me, so a little jail time was what I got.

I followed Chyna's and Mama's voices to the kitchen where they stood talking. Chyna smiled when she saw me and reached out her arms.

"Come give me a hug, my little jailbird sister. I apologize for not bein' here for you, but I was involved in some other mess that I couldn't get out of. You forgive me, don't you?"

"Of course I do," I said, hugging Chyna. "And ain't no need to apologize to me. That shit was all on me, as was what had happened at the club. You can't always be there for me when trouble ensues, but I do appreciate you, girl. Now, what kind of mess did you happen to get yourself into?"

"It's a long story, but right now, I need a cold shower and somethin' to eat. I need a long nap too, but I'll wait until later. We'll talk about my situation after my shower, okay?"

I told Chyna that was cool and she headed to her room. Mama stood listening to us then she opened the fridge. "Ain't shit in here to eat. I'm going to the grocery store. I'll be back in a bit. Have you talked to Karrine?"

"I did earlier. She said that she'll be home later."

"Where is she?"

I shrugged my shoulders. "She didn't say."

"See if you can get her on the phone. Tell her I'm cooking dinner and I want all of us to sit down and eat together. It's been hectic around here. We need to squash a lot of this shit that is going on and get our acts together."

I couldn't agree with Mama more. There was a lot going on, way more than what we needed. After she left, I called Karrine, but she didn't answer her phone. I left a message for her to call back.

Chyna was in the bathroom, so I hurried back into my room to see if there were any more pop-up messages from my stalker. There were. This time,

the bastard from the other side referred to me by
my real name.

Simone, where are you? You used to
be my Black Satin, but now you're just a
fucking whore. I want to cut your throat and
watch you bleed. But before I do that, I'm
going to fuck your brains out and make you
pay for all of the hurt that you've caused
me. Bitch, are you there?

I didn't bother to reply, but I damn sure
wanted to. If I responded, that would mean that
he had control of this situation. I didn't want
him to think that he did. I couldn't wait until
tonight, just so I could get a feel from some of
my regular clients who seemed infatuated with
me. There was a possibility that it could be one
of them, too, so I had to keep my eyes open and
pay attention.

Then again, what if it was Mama trying to
see what I would do in a situation like this?
She pulled that shit on me with Honey, so why
wouldn't she try something like this? I hoped
like hell that it was her behind the messages, because this shit was real creepy. I surely wanted
to call and ask her, but what if she wasn't behind
this? That would worry her and keep her all up
in my business. She already knew too much, and

I figured that I could handle this little problem on my own. If things got out of hand, I would go to Chyna before I ever went to Mama.

Chyna came into my room, and when she shared with me what had happened today, my mouth was wide open the whole time. I couldn't believe it, and boy did me and my sisters know how to make a mess of things. I figured all along that Chyna had been seeing somebody, but this secretive bullshit that we had been doing, it didn't seem to pay off for none of us. First Reno, now Marc. They both deserved that shit, though. It was a pleasure to see Reno get what was coming to him.

I was too embarrassed when we got to that nigga's house. How could I allow a nigga like that to be my first? The times that I'd gone to his apartment it was always dark. His bedroom was always dim; I guessed to try to hide the filthiness. I could always smell something funky in the air, but what attracted me to Reno was his bad-boy attributes.

I had a thing for bad boys who stayed in trouble. That was my downfall. But after what Chyna had told me what had happened with her today, niggas were the last thing on my mind. If I didn't see them on my computer screen, then I wouldn't see them at all. At least for a long while anyway.

Either way, Chyna and I agreed that this secretive bullshit didn't pay off. But it wasn't like it was going to stop, because there I was keeping a secret about the messages I'd been getting. I truly wanted to handle this on my own, and for now, I didn't think it was necessary to involve Chyna. Deep down, she was probably going through hell after what had happened. I couldn't put more bullshit on her plate, and as a matter of fact, I wouldn't. Maybe the motherfucker would get sick of bothering me and leave me the fuck alone.

Until then, I was limiting my time away from home and my car was staying right in the driveway. If I needed something, I'd send Chyna or Karrine to get it for me. It had to be that way for now, until I figured out how to deal with my stalker.

Mama had fried some chicken, buttered some corn on the cob, and whipped some potatoes. Chyna made a chocolate cake, and we stood at the table, putting gobs of chocolate icing on the cake.

"That's too much," Mama said, standing behind the counter, looking at us lick our fingers like we did when we were little girls.

"It's not too much to me," I said. "And I don't mind cheating every now and then. All this week, I've had nothin' but veggies and shrimp. A little chocolate cake, sometimes, does a sexy body good."

"This cake definitely will, no doubt," Chyna said, laughing.

We were almost done with icing the cake. Mama brought the food over to the table, and after we took our seats, she inquired about Karrine again.

"She never called me back," I said. "But I'm sure she will."

Mama didn't respond. We held hands as she blessed the food. All of us threw down, and once dinner was over, Chyna said that she needed some rest, so she hit the sack. Mama said that she would be back later or tomorrow, and like always, she rarely told us where she was going. After she jetted, I was back in my room, reading the new message from my stalker:

In less than two days, bitch, you die!

My heart raced. For the first time in a long time, I was scared.

Chapter Eighteen

Karrine

I paced the floor in Honey's guest bedroom, thinking about my situation. In no way did I want to seem like the daughter who didn't know how to follow the rules, or the sister who turned her back on the others. But I was sick of this shit. After seeing Mama kill Reno right before my eyes, I just couldn't do it anymore. She definitely didn't have to go there. This shit was starting to become too easy for her.

I understood the situation with Ray, but with Reno, Simone shouldn't have lied about being with him. She and Chyna should have moved in another direction at the club and left that motherfucker alone.

When the police came to the house to question us, Simone should have kept her mouth shut and Chyna should have been there. Mama should have been there too, but I was the one left to answer for what they had done. The police grilled the shit out of me. Then everybody acted as if it was my fault that Simone went to jail. Mama had the nerve to question me, but what in the fuck was I supposed to do? Simone was grown and needed to learn how to keep her mouth closed sometimes.

I was so mad right now. The only person I could turn to was Honey. I knew he and Mama were close, but I still spilled my guts to him. I told him everything I was feeling. I didn't give a damn if he shared any of it with Mama. He said that he wouldn't, and there was a part of me that believed him. Why? Because I was starting to trust him. My gut said no, but maybe it was lying to me. I didn't have anything to lose either way, so I took his word when he said he would keep his mouth shut. He told me to stay at his place for a couple of days to get my head straight. The days had come and gone, and I was no better off now than I was when I walked through his front door, telling him my problems. There wasn't a chance in hell that my problems would go away. I felt stuck in a situation that I wouldn't be able to depart from anytime soon, unless I ran away and never came back.

A part of me didn't want to do that because I would miss the hell out of Simone and Chyna. I would miss Mama too, but she just wasn't right. No matter how much I tried to convince myself that she was, I knew, deep down, that Mama's issues would wind up destroying all of us. She would never allow us to be free of her. We'd always have to play by her rules. I didn't want to play by her rules, and I was old enough to play by my own. And the more I thought about running away from it all, the better it started to sound.

I put on my jeans and a wife beater with no bra on, before leaving the room to go find Honey. As I stood outside of the door to his office, I could hear him talking to someone on speakerphone. I put my ear against the door and recognized the voice as being Mama's.

"You should have seen that fool," she said, referring to Reno. "That was a long time coming, and I blame you for not handling that fool when you had a chance to."

"I know I should have, but I was trying to give that nigga the benefit of the doubt. You know how I do it."

"I do know, and you need to stop being so soft and having sympathy for these niggas who be stealing from us. If you add up all of the money that has been stolen from us over the years, it accounts for a lot. Too much, as a matter of fact, and I don't like that shit, Honey."

"I feel you. I promise you that I will not allow another muthafucka to get down like that. I'm sorry that you had to deal with Reno, but I'm not sorry about that fool Marc. You and Chyna did what y'all had to do."

"You damn right we did. She had to learn what kind of nigga he was for herself. That nigga broke my baby's heart, but she needed to handle that, not me."

"Well, you kind of handled it when you went and told her what was up with him. I can't believe he asked her to marry him, and his ass was already married. Some niggas just don't have no shame in their game. I'm just glad Chyna saw the light."

"Yeah, she saw the light when he punched her in her goddamn face. But go ahead and give a shout-out to her Mama who needs a little praises sometimes. Y'all muthafuckas be thinking I'm crazy, but I do all of this shit out of love. Now, where is that bitch Karrine at? I know she's been over there with you. I'm trying to keep my cool about this situation, Honey, but you know I don't like it one bit."

"I know you don't, Mama, but Karrine just came here to chill. Ain't no fucking or anything like that been going on between us. All she came here to do was talk."

"Talk? Talk about what? What a terrible mother I've been? How she's tired of me doing this and that? I'm sure you've heard it all, and to be quite frank, I'm sick of the bitch bad-mouthing me, especially after all that I do for her ass."

"She don't be always badmouthing you, but I'll just say, as I've said plenty of times before, that she has some concerns with you. Karrine don't have the same blood running through her like Chyna and Simone do, so she's a little . . . different, if you know what I mean. Don't be so hard on her; but if she keeps on badmouthing you, as you say, what do you want me to do about it?"

"I want you to do what I would have you do to anybody else who badmouths your mama who makes you an extremely wealthy man. Kill the bitch, clean up the mess, and save the tears for another funeral."

Honey had the audacity to laugh. I didn't see a goddamn thing funny. I took that shit personally. How dare Mama speak some ill shit like that?

I waited for her and Honey to end their call. Yet again, every time they spoke, I learned something new. What was all this money shit she was talking about, and how did Reno get involved in this? I had been out of the loop for too long. I stormed into Honey's office, demanding some answers.

"You need to tell me what is really goin' on with you and Mama right now, Honey. What's this I hear about money, Reno, Marc, and about you killing me?"

Honey moved from side to side in his swivel chair then put his hands behind his head. "If I tell you about all of this, I may have to kill you for real." He laughed, but yet again, I didn't see shit funny.

"Don't say that shit to me, nigga. Tell me what the fuck is going on. After you do, then I guess we may have to let the chips fall where they may."

I stood in front of Honey's desk as he began to tell me about his connection with Mama, and about her being the mastermind behind the massive drug dealing ring that he was running, per her request. I stood in shock as he told me about the numerous killings, the connection with Reno, and about what had happened earlier with Marc and Chyna.

"So you see, baby girl," Honey said, "yo' mama has a lot on her plate. You need to chill with some of this stuff you be talking and think real hard about getting with the program. What you think is always about you, it ain't. And running won't solve any of your problems, so you need to get that shit out of yo' head. Just think about what I'm saying to you, all right? Think real hard and stop acting like a fucking brat."

My faced was scrunched. I frowned and hissed at Honey. "Is that what you think I am? A brat? No, Honey, I'm the only sensible muthafucka in this family; that's who I am. I'm not down with none of this shit! You got me fucked up if you think I'm going to get with the program and keep my mouth shut. I'm not! I'm gon' run as far away from y'all as I can. So kiss my ass and have a wonderful fucking life kissing Mama's ass and being her goddamn puppet!"

I turned to walk away, and when Honey called my name, I snapped my head to the side. My eyes came in contact with the gun he held in his hand, aimed at me.

"Whatever Mama wants," he said with a serious expression on his face, "she gets."

Honey pulled the trigger. The bullet hit me somewhere. I couldn't feel where because my entire body was numb. I remembered crashing to the floor, and after my eyes fluttered a few times, my deep breaths slowed. Then, darkness was upon me.